Gillian Morgan

LUCY WALTER

PUBLISHED BY BERLLAN BOOKS

Published by
Berllan Books,
Y Berllan, 1 Redhill Park,
Crowhill, Haverfordwest,
Dyfed, SA61 1XX.

ISBN 0-9516923-0-5

*Printed in Wales by
Dynevor Printing Company,
Rawlings Road,
Llandybïe, Dyfed.*

Bold, brown and beautiful,
wild and wanton

Acknowledgements

I would like to thank the Dynevor Printing Company for their support and encouragement. My special thanks to Messrs. Donald Martin and Eddie John.

Chapter 1

It was the eyes that told him, those golden brown pellucid pools that hinted at the first stirrings of passion. Only thirteen years old, yet Lucy Walter was already aware of her powers of attraction and he was sure she had many admirers. He had seen that look in other eyes, but never before in one so young. He hesitated only a second before acknowledging the challenge that lay behind them. Holding her gaze a fraction longer than was necessary, he gave a half bow, indicating with a slight turn of his head the old ruin where a holy hermit was reputed to have lived on nothing but air and water all his life. Without waiting to see her reaction, he turned swiftly and strode across the cliff top, the purple bells of the heather swaying gently in the early morning breeze. In the distance, he could hear the sound of the breakers, crashing and roaring over the pebbles on Newgale beach, but his mind was on the girl. If she followed him, he was right. If she did not follow him he was still correct in his assumption that there was more to Mistress Lucy than her demure appearance suggested.

A light footstep and a snapping twig made him catch his breath. Without turning, he called softly, 'Follow me and don't look back.'

When he was sure they were out of sight of prying eyes, he turned and held his hand out to her and led her into the ruin. Spreading his cloak on the ground, he sat down and she joined him.

'Lucy, Mistress Lucy,' he murmured, taking her fingertips and brushing his lips against them. A faint flush spread from her throat to her cheeks as their eyes met in the thin light of morning. Allowing his eyes to roam over her he saw the rounded shape of her young body, the already wide, woman's hips, accentuated by the folds of her muslin dress, the luminous quality of her skin. Although not fully a woman, she was ready to be plucked from her mother's apron strings and he had made up his mind about one thing: he was the man who would pluck her first.

Richard Palmer was too good a horseman to rush a young filly. On riding a young mare on her first outing, he always took things gently, allowing her to find her own pace. An experienced rider, he had early learnt to be patient. In the best circles Sir Richard was known as a lady's man, a title he would not quarrel with. Six feet tall, with golden ringlets cascading onto the starched, ruffled collar that the maids had laboured so lovingly on with hot irons, a wide belt adorning his narrow hips, he presented a profile handsome as any Greek god's. He was a practised charmer and had yet to meet the woman who had the will to deny him. Popularly called a man of the world, Sir Richard had enjoyed the pleasures of love whenever the opportunities had presented themselves, which meant that he made frequent appearances in some of the best boudoirs in London. Indeed, he was the firm favourite of many society ladies, single or otherwise.

Palmer's policy of seeing the ladies took their pleasure first, meant that he rarely found himself short of a beautiful woman's company but, turning his gaze on Lucy, he realized that he had come across a special gem. The rays of the early sun turned the loosely knotted bunch of hair at the nape of her neck into strands of liquid silk and the stray curls caressing her cheeks emphasized the young plumpness of her face. Not since his youth had he been with a girl this young and he was now twenty seven years old.

'I know you have come to live in Henllys Fawr, but

where did you live before that?' Lucy's voice, when she spoke, was low and musical, pleasing to the ear.

He laughed. 'You are like all women, wanting to know everything. I shall tell you, to satisfy your curiosity. I lived in that area of London known as Greenwich, but when my uncle died he left me his farm and I decided to come and live here for a few years, or as long as I like it, and see if the life of a country gentleman suits me.'

'And do you think it will suit you?' Lucy asked.

Glancing at her, his eyes twinkling he replied, 'I think it will suit me very well. I have read all the stories in the 'Mabinogion' and if Dyfed is the land of enchantment, where mists swirl up and carry whole kingdoms away and ladies ride horses that cannot be overtaken, I do not think I will ever want to leave.'

Privately, he thanked chance for having been out riding on the cliff top that morning, when he met Lucy, leading her pony between the gorse bushes, looking for gulls' eggs.

Suddenly, a toad appeared and jumped over Lucy's foot, startling her, so that she drew closer to Palmer. Instantly, his arms encircled her waist and, gently, he cradled her closer to him. It was this tenderness, an intrinsic part of his nature, that made him so endearing to women. 'Are you frightened, my little pet?' he murmured into her fragrant hair. The incident had the fortunate effect of bringing them physically close and he was reluctant to relinquish his advantage. Settling himself against a fallen tree trunk, his arms tightened around her, aware that their two hearts were beating rapidly; he knew what was causing his to race and hoped hers was fluttering for the same reason.

The stillness was broken by a fox chasing a rabbit. Palmer cradled Lucy's head in the curve of his arm, stroking her hair till she lay still and quiet in his arms. She was like a little kitten, anxious to please, anxious to play, but too nervous to do either. He was conscious of the sense of the unknown she felt and knew one false move on his part could mean that he would lose her.

'An old Tom is best with a young Queen,' he remembered a cat fancier saying. His hands reached out to feel the dewy freshness of her cheeks and he smoothed them lightly. Still she did not stir, but he could bide his time and she would be worth waiting for.

'Do I frighten you?' he murmured into the still air. For answer, she pulled his head down, till her lips pressed against his and her arms circled his neck.

Her mouth beneath his was cool and delicious and set his senses reeling. Every instinct in him wanted to crush her body to his, squeeze her freshness until it became a part of him, meld his body into hers. He loosened the ribbons from her hair and smelt its warm perfume as it cascaded like a shimmering waterfall. Her innocence and beauty were delightful. Running his fingers through her hair, he sought out her perfectly shaped head. She came from good stock, that he knew. There was a fine pedigree on both her dam and sire's side, but that of her mother's was superior to her father's, or so it was said.

Elizabeth Protheroe, Lucy's mother, was a niece of John Vaughan, first Earl of Carbery. Golden Grove and all its farms and lands were his to command. It was thanks to this John Vaughan that the Royalist troops were billeted at Roch Castle.

Of William Walter's political sympathies he was unsure; the man was a dark horse. Coming from English descent, William Walter's great, great grandfather had found favour with Henry VII and had been appointed approver of the lordships of Pembrokeshire and West Haverford. So well had this Walter carried out his duties that the resulting fortune, passed down to Lucy's father, should have enabled him to keep his family in some comfort, but this was not the case. Loose talk had it that the man was on the verge of being penniless. Furthermore, it was said he was dissolute. It was whispered that Elizabeth's duties were made more tiresome by having to care for two bastards, the results of her husbands's philanderings with one of the kitchen maids.

pulled him to her. It was of the utmost importance that he did not show her the full extent of his passion at this juncture, lest he frighten her with his ardour. He had been right to allow her to take her time, to dictate the pace and she became insistent now, urging him on to the moment that would take her to the threshold of new delights from which there would be no return, changing her forever from the child she had been to the woman she would now become.

He was gentle as a lamb with her, holding her tightly, steadying her with his strong arms till all the shooting stars in the world had gathered inside her and exploded in one overwhelming burst of rapture and delight.

After the ecstasy that had tossed and shaken her and left her lying limp and stranded like a helpless starfish on the shore when the tide has gone out, they clung together. The sun rose in the sky, silent witness to their love. Only the wind, sighing and moaning through the bushes, whispered their secret to the awakening world.

And so it was, in that remote part of Pembrokeshire with the Holy See of Saint David's to the west and the mystical mountains of Presely outlining the northern skyline, that Lucy Walter left behind her maidenhood and drank the wine of love to the lees. It proved to be an intoxicating draught, one that she never entirely lost the taste for. There would be other loves for both of them, but neither forgot the magic of their first encounter.

The next day, Lucy Walter looked out on the golden strands of cloud floating above Roch Castle. It was the same landscape, the same fields that she saw. Nothing had altered externally, only her perception of the world had changed. In the distance, the gorse blooms dazzled and she remembered the saying that when gorse was out of bloom, kissing was out of season.

She fingered the golden ear-ring that Richard Palmer had taken from his ear and placed between her breasts the previous day, when at last the shudders of ecstasy had died down within her. Lucy had strung it on a silken thread and wore it round her throat, where it would remain until the day she died.

Chapter 2

The sun was climbing high in the sky as Richard Palmer rode to West Haverford on the day following his encounter with Mistress Lucy Walter. What he had told Lucy about his background and inheritance was true, but he had been careful not to reveal he was a spy in the pay of the King. Soon, he was hoping to leave Pembrokeshire and fight for King Charles I, but, first, he was going to the Great Fair of Saint Thomas the Martyr to buy ten strong horses for Captain Francis Edwards and the Cavaliers garrisoned at Roch Castle.

When he arrived at Portfield Common he sought shade for his horse, where he watered and rested him after the long ride from Roch. As the horse drank deeply, Palmer looked around him. A fiddler was scraping a merry tune while some buxom girls and dark skinned youths jigged awkwardly to the music, the sweat pouring off their faces. Zounds! But it was good to see people enjoying themselves despite the repression of Noll Cromwell's men, and these Welsh certainly knew how to do that. There was too much drabness in the world without the miserable Puritans making things worse.

He was just finishing the last crumbs of a slab of gingerbread, when he became aware of someone close by. Turning on his heel swiftly, he sought out his pistol, expecting to see a pickpocket. His face relaxed when he saw one of those whores who were never far from these gatherings. The girl was about eighteen years of age and she flashed him a black toothed smile. 'Do you want a nice time, Sir?'

Bowing gallantly and flourishing his hat, he replied gravely, 'Not now, madam, I am here on business, but I thank you kindly.'

Finding some loose change in his pocket, he handed the coins to her. 'Perhaps you will accept this little gift?'

She seemed well pleased and bobbed a curtsey before taking her leave. 'Not now', he thought, as he saw her approaching someone else, not now with the memory of Lucy still hot in his groins. That reminded him, he must buy Lucy some trinkets before the day was over.

As he made his way to where the horses were tethered, a pedlar leapt out in front of him.

'A bauble for your lady, Sir,' he cried, slyness writ large in every crease of his face. Palmer was about to brush him off when his eye alighted on the string of amber beads the rogue was holding up to the light. Glinting bronze and gold, beautiful as autumn leaves, they reminded him of Lucy's eyes, dappled like a stream in the setting rays of the afternoon sun.

'And who did you steal those from?' he asked brusquely.

'Steal, good Sir, never,' replied the rascal in mock surprise. 'You do me a dishonour. I am lately come from Saint Paul's Fair, at Bristol, where a lady of most noble birth has fallen on hard times and has asked me to sell some of her jewels for her.'

A likely story, thought Palmer.

'How much?' he snapped.

The man named his price, but the coins Palmer threw him were less than he had asked for.

'Take it or leave it,' said Palmer tersely, but the man took them, biting the coins with the blackened stumps of his teeth, to see if they were genuine.

'Swallow them, you devil,' shouted Palmer, pocketing the beads. 'I have given you a better price than you deserve.'

Palmer liked the look of the man from the Gwaun Valley,

who was the most notable horse dealer there that day. The horses appeared like their master, quiet and dependable. Soon he had chosen the horses, struck a good bargain with the man, and with a 'Diolch yn fawr', handed over a quantity of gold coins. This was met by a reciprocal 'Diolch yn fawr, Syr', and a slight bow from the Welshman. Well, thought Palmer, it was generally held that the north of the county was true to the King, and if this man's behaviour was anything to go by, the assumption must be correct.

A group of ragged boys was hired to ride the horses to Roch. Long shadows fell across the road as the party left Haverford behind. Palmer was in no rush; there was no point in tiring the horses needlessly. The riders fell into a companionable silence as they rode along, the dying rays of the sun illuminating each speck of dust kicked up by the horses, shining off their rippling flanks, warming the backs of the men.

'You boys can have a night's lodgings if you have no objections to sleeping in the haystack,' said Palmer jovially.

One of the more intelligent looking boys rode up alongside Palmer.

'It's Roch Castle we are heading for, Sir?'

'Aye, that's right. Have you been there before?'

'No, but I hear tell 'tis the home of William Walter, brother of Richard Walter. Is that right, Sir?'

'I do believe it is. Why do you ask?'

'Nothing, Sir, but 'tis known that Richard Walter has persecuted the Quakers who met in Goat Street and had the rich burgesses committed, Sir. Edward Lloyd and his wife, Mary, Jenkin Evan and Young Morgan.'

The boy rattled on, prattling like a woman, Palmer only half listening. Local knowledge was useful and not to be ignored, as any scout knew, but at the moment his thoughts were on how good it was to be alive, to be young and fancy free. He had learnt not to take things too seriously, for they were living in uncertain times. On a whim he addressed the boy, 'And of what faith are you?'

'Oh, I keep the true faith, Sir.'

'I see. You are true to Rome. 'Tis well to have faith, boy, but not so much that it makes a man too lily livered to fight for a cause.'

Palmer looked for Lucy when he had settled the horses and boys comfortably for the night. Elizabeth had been watching her daughter closely these last few months, ever since the troops had been garrisoned at Roch and she had seen the looks Lucy had aroused on the faces of the men. The girl was little more than a child, but she was growing quickly and she was strong willed. Elizabeth would have to be vigilant and see her daughter came to no harm.

Palmer was making a final check of the horses and was walking back through the garden when he heard a pebble drop. Looking up, he saw a shadowy figure by a lancet window and knew, even before he had seen her, that it was Lucy. She leaned forward to speak, and her voice was urgent.

'I leave for Haverford tomorrow and thence to London. My father has a house near the backside of Covent Garden. I am to be sent to stay with him for a few weeks, and Justus, too,' she said, referring to her younger brother.

'Lucy, come down. I will wait for you by the apple orchard.' His voice was filled with urgency and she longed to go to him, but she feared the old nurse might be watching her.

'I do not know I can. Mother has grown so fussy of late.'

'Please,' he pleaded, then added slyly, 'I have something for you from the fair.'

It was more than she could resist.

'Just for a few minutes,' he said, needlessly, but she was already on her way.

Outside, under the leafy boughs, he pressed the beads into her hands. 'For the queen of my heart,' he whispered into her ear. 'Wear the necklace often and, when you do, remember me.' Lucy was worth a king's ransom, that he knew, but these poor beads were all that the youngest son of a youngest son was able to give her. With the state of the country as it was at the moment, they were all he was ever likely to afford, too.

First he kissed her lips, then, pulling her bodice low, he kissed the shell pink tips of the nipples. He moved to her eyelids and the taste of her moist, salty tears on his tongue surprised him.

'Why do you cry, my little Lucy?'

'I cry for I may not see you for many months.'

'Or ever again,' he thought to himself; there was a time to speak and a time for staying silent, which he did now. They were living in dangerous times and a man could be here today but dead tomorrow. He wrapped his cloak tightly around the two of them and gave her the gentlest goodbye kiss he knew how to. She seemed to take comfort from the closeness of their bodies. He was wise enough to know that war and circumstance would inevitably mean that he would lose his Lucy. He would seek relief in other bodies, but he would not forget his little Pembrokeshire filly, who would always remain a special memory in his heart. Although he longed for her with all his heart this night, he had to report to the Captain regarding the purchase of the horses and then courtesy demanded that he drink a mulled cup for an hour or two. The pleasures of love were fleeting but a man had always to keep his career in mind.

Lucy arose early the next morning. She viewed her departure to London with regret, mostly because she would be leaving her passionate lover behind. It was said that much jollity was to he had in London, despite the killjoy ways of the Puritans. She wrinkled her nose wryly. Little gaiety would come the way of herself and Justus if Marie, their governess, had anything to do with it. Still, she thought, as she cleaned her teeth with an ivory toothpick then rinsed her mouth in a mixture of vinegar, rosemary and myrrh, there might be ways of escaping from the clutches of their old nurse occasionally.

Before taking breakfast she would say her morning

prayers in church, by herself. She crossed the road to the little church of La Saynte Marye and entered through the Lych Gate. The air was heavy with the morning mist and thick droplets of dew hung from the blue harebells in the grass. As she pushed open the heavy wooden door, the smell of old wood and old stones assailed her nostrils. The darkness was brightened by the vivid stained glass windows and she stopped by the one showing Jesus, the Good Shepherd. It had always been her favourite. She looked again at the Lamb and the jewel-like primroses surrounding the central figure. As a child she had whiled away dreary services imagining herself playing in a beautiful meadow, studded with flowers and frolicking lambs. She turned away; she had left the age of innocence behind and was standing on the threshold of a different world. Although Lucy did not know it, from now on she would see little more of her home in Pembrokeshire and the church of La Saynte Marye. The prospect of weeks in London lay before her and perhaps it was as well that she knew little of the traps and pitfalls the city held for a young girl. True, she would not be alone for her nurse would be there as well as her father but, her nurse being old and her father being feckless, she might as well have been alone in the world for all the protection they were likely to afford her.

Lucy made a light breakfast of bread and ale then arose from the table to see the travelling carriage being brought around to the main entrance. Dafydd, one of their most trusted servants, was to drive them on the long journey to London, accompanied by his son John.

As the men loaded the bags into the wagon, Elizabeth turned anxious eyes towards her daughter. Standing petting the horses in her new blue linen gown, Elizabeth could not deny that Lucy was already a beauty who would attract male attention in London, or anywhere she might go. Elizabeth had never felt an overwhelming love for her first born, who had been strong-willed from babyhood. There was now a wanton quality about Lucy that troubled her and, combined with her wilfulness, who knew where it would lead her? In her heart, she could admit that there were things about Lucy that she disliked intensely and yet, she did not wish for harm to come to the girl. She struggled to rationalise the fears that fought within her now. London was full of men ready to take advantage of a young girl, but she would be under the protection of Marie, her old nurse, who truly loved the child. Yet Elizabeth knew full well that Marie was no match for Lucy if she was in a determined mood. Then again, her father would be there, but Elizabeth knew he viewed the children as nothing but an encumbrance. Besides, when he was not petitioning Parliament he would be seeking out his own pleasures. What Lucy did would be no concern of his. Elizabeth could stop Lucy from going, but she would be glad to be rid of the girl for a few weeks and, anyway, she did not want Lucy growing up to believe that Roch was the centre of the universe. No, there was a wider life to be had in London and perhaps it would do the girl some good to see how people in polite society behaved, learn to mix with her own class, come to understand some of the ways of a world far away from Pembrokeshire. If Lucy had been the daughter of a fair to middling farmer, Elizabeth thought with a sigh, then her life might have been a lot easier. All she would be expected to do would be to learn to churn butter, make cream, train the servants to her ways, organize the still room, then marry the son of a prosperous farmer and have a large family. Still, she mused, at least her time in London might help her make a wise choice of husband when she returned. Elizabeth did not want her daughter to marry the first Pembrokeshire lad who asked her. There were always her Barlow cousins of Slebech, of course, and it would not displease Elizabeth if Lucy were to make a marriage with one of them.

Justus, who was to go to London with his sister, had already climbed into the carriage and was settling back into his seat. Looking at the boy, Elizabeth felt a surge of love for her son. Wilful like his sister, perhaps, she had always found his temperament more open, less guileful. A few years ago and his future had seemed assured as a country squire, but now, who could tell what would happen with civil war ravaging the country. With his father's profligate ways, there might be no inheritance at all for him. She gave an involuntary shudder at the thought. The cost of garrisoning the troops at Roch Castle was high, and she knew her husband was to petition Parliament for three thousand pound towards the expense. A richer man would not have bothered. Advancing the Kings's cause at this time could mean a baronetcy, or more, if a happy outcome arose and the King vanquished the Roundheads.

'Take care of the children, Marie,' said Elizabeth, seeing the bustling figure of the old nurse coming out of the castle. Marie had nursed Lucy as a baby, and their joint concern for Justus and Lucy had united the two women.

'They'll come to no harm with me, my lady,' said the nurse. 'I'll not let them out of my sight.' Lowering her voice, she turned to Elizabeth and said: 'Especially Mistress Lucy. She's coming to that age now . . .' Her sentence hung in the air. 'I'll watch the girl well.'

Elizabeth leaned inside the carriage to kiss her children God speed. It was with a mixture of relief and regret that she saw the carriage clatter down the narrow, twisting lane from the castle to join the stream of oxen carts and carriages going to market in West Haverford.

Lucy settled back in her seat with an air of resignation. At least London could not possibly be as dull as Roch. Why, she had heard ladies could take a walk in Saint James's Park and although the dreary Puritans had closed the theatres, great dinners were held at night where much feasting and merriment took place. What diversions there would be for her and Justus, Lucy could only guess at, but at least they would be away from their mother, and their father would hardly be a restraining force, so busy would he be entertaining his lady friends.

They were entering the town of Haverford, now, travelling along City Road. The sun was hot and the stench of the town caused Lucy to bury her head in her nosegay. A great crowd of people was gathered on the Old Bridge and the carriage was forced to a stop.

'Make way, make way,' shouted Dafydd, who was driving the carriage, but to no avail. Turning to speak to the occupants of the carriage, he called, 'There's nothing for it, but to stop. They are waiting for something and no one is going to clear a path for us for a while.'

A strange hush had fallen over the assembled crowd, and the passengers in the carriage strained to see what the crowd was ogling at. Marie leaned her head out then hastily sat back in her seat with a gasp. 'Marie, what is it?' cried Lucy in consternation.

'Don't look, child, don't look,' pleaded the old woman, but it was to no avail, for Lucy was already halfway out of the carriage, determined to see what had upset her old nurse so. Coming along the road was a sight that set a tremor running through Lucy's body. Disgust, horror and pity mingled, for it was a sight that turned the stomachs of strong men and gave the most sensible of women nightmares that never left them.

A woman of middling age was walking along the road, stripped naked to the waist. She was of medium height, with long hair that had not yet lost all its colour. On either side of her were two louts, each brandishing a stick with which they beat her from time to time. Blood had already been drawn and was beginning to cake and dry in the hot sun.

'Lucy, come here, come to your nurse,' said Marie, desperately speaking to Lucy as she had when she was a child. She wrapped her arms around Lucy, trying to bury her head in her shoulders, but it was in vain. 'Dafydd, can't the wagon be moved at all?' asked Marie helplessly.

'There's nothing we can do for the moment. They'll soon pass and then we'll be on our way.'

Lucy spoke now, and Marie marvelled at the steady tone

of her voice. 'Dafydd, why does no one stop them — what are they doing to this poor woman?'

A man came forward then, having heard Lucy's question.

'It's her punishment, my lady. A common thief she is. Stole a good flannel petticoat from her neighbour, she did. She's been convicted at the Sessions, and she's to be whipped through the streets of Harford. Deserves all she's getting. Don't you trouble yourself over her.' The crowd had started to jeer now and the woman stopped to hurl insults at them, beads of sweat breaking over her face, her hair a tangled mass. She cried in her anger, and railed and swore at her tormentors, but she was magnificent in her defiance. A sharp blow across the shoulders caused her to trip and fall, but soon she was on her feet again.

At last the sorry spectacle passed by and the crowds began to drift towards the market place. Lucy was quiet a long while after that and Marie wished with all her heart she could have saved the child from that haunting sight.

As the carriage left the town, Lucy turned to take one last look. The Quay was bobbing with boats from many different lands. She could just make out the name of the 'Le Jesu', registered at Milford Haven. Lucy remembered Elizabeth saying she was expecting a shipment of Gascony wine, but cared not if it failed to arrive. With the soldiers billeted at Roch, any delivery of wine would surely be requisitioned by them and charged to Elizabeth.

Soon they were bowling along the Carmarthen road. Elizabeth had arranged for them to rest for a few hours in Nantyrhebog, with her relatives, before they continued on their long journey.

Chapter 3

If Lucy had expected more gaiety than in Wales, she was not altogether disappointed by London. Although the mornings were tedious, when Justus laboured over his Latin lessons with his tutor and Lucy stitched her sampler, the afternoons were free and these were the times Lucy enjoyed the most. Under the watchful eye of Marie, they would explore the area surrounding their house in Kinge Street. Always they stopped in one of the many bakers' shops that abounded nearby to buy chelsea buns or maids of honours for their tea.

Walking through the streets that afternoon with Marie and Justus they passed a group of swaggering Cavaliers, loud in their conversation and bold in their stares. Passing Lucy, they turned to look. Even among the London beauties, Lucy was an uncommonly comely girl, not beautiful in the conventional sense, but possessing a magnetism no man could ignore. 'Come, Mistress Lucy,' said Marie anxiously, seeing Lucy looking intensely at the soldiers.

Lucy followed obediently. It was no good. Palmer was not one of their number. Lucy had learnt recently that Palmer had joined the Cavaliers and he was so often in her thoughts that whenever she saw a King's man with golden locks, tall with narrow hips, her heart skipped a beat.

Every night, alone in her bedroom, she held the amber beads in her hands and looked out over the London skyline, westwards to Pembrokeshire. When she closed her eyes she remembered the feel of his arms around her, the insistence of his mouth and the rapture she had felt after his loving. She wept now and then when she thought of him, but the remembrance was the sweetest of agonies.

It was a grave William Walter who called Marie to his library that evening.

'The news from Pembrokeshire is bad. Roch Castle has been taken by the Parliamentarians. They have smoked out the Cavaliers and burnt the Castle.' He sighed deeply.

Marie's thoughts were whirling in her head. Though Walter's sympathies lay with the Parliamentarians, he could not afford to build another Castle. Yet, Marie felt little pity for him; she feared for the life of Elizabeth most of all.

'What of my mistress, Sir?' she enquired with bated breath.

'Safe,' replied Walter curtly, unwilling to say more about his estranged wife.

'Was she in the Castle when the attack took place?' Marie persisted.

Diabolo, but these old Welsh women could be insistent.

'No, she was not in the Castle when the attack took place, Madam.'

'Where was she?'

The woman was beginning to annoy him. Was it not enough for her that Elizabeth Walter was safe?

'Mistress Walter was in Dynefor, Llandeilo, visiting her mother, when the attack occurred. And it is to Dynefor that Lucy and Justus will return when your stay in London is over. That is all you need to know for the present,' he said, dismissing her with a curt nod. He had worries enough, without the need for being cross-questioned about the safety of his estranged wife. He had shown Parliament the colour of his coat and there was no doubt that his loyalties lay with the Cromwellian cause, yet he must have restitution for the Castle. He was not a rich man by any means. The time had come to petition Parliament mightily.

Marie spent a restless night. It was common knowledge

that there was no love left between Eliza and William. Wenching was all he was good for. He was a faithless man who seemed unwilling and unable to make proper financial provision for his family. It was as well his wife had her high-born relatives to cushion her life, or else what would become of her and the children?

Next morning, Marie explained, as gently as she was able, to Lucy and Justus that they would not be returning to Pembrokeshire, but to Dynefor.

'The castle is in need of some repair, so we will all be more comfortable in Llandeilo.' She made no mention of the attack and the fire, and her explanation seemed to satisfy her charges.

After Justus had finished his morning Latin lesson and Lucy had made a half-hearted attempt at her needlework, they sat down to their dinner. It was a fish day and the cook had broiled some cod, which she served with an oyster sauce. Marie looked at the table, but felt no appetite. The cook was a conscientious woman and had laid the table with a clean linen cloth, good pewter plates and some fine Venetian drinking glasses. The news from Wales had been disturbing, but she must try not to convey her anxiety to Lucy and Justus. As she watched them eating, she was relieved to see they had not left their good appetites behind in Pembrokeshire. Lucy and her brother finished the pudding-pie of biffins, cream, eggs and loaf sugar between them. If they noticed that their governess was not herself, they did not show it, and Marie was grateful for that.

'We will not go out this afternoon,' Marie said, at length. She did not feel up to their high spirits. 'Justus, you can go to your room and study your astronomy books and Lucy, you can work on your sampler, or perhaps you might like to play the virginal.'

The brother and sister said nothing, but looked at each other out of the corners of their eyes.

Marie shut herself in her darkened room for the rest of the afternoon. Justus already knew what he was going to do with himself: he had heard talk in the kitchen, from the scullery boy, that there were dog fights that afternoon, and he meant to go and watch.

Only Lucy did not know what she might do to while away the tedious hours. Sitting down by her attic window, she looked across the rooftops of Covent Garden and Saint Giles. She knew that fashionable society and many members of the Court circle lived in the houses round about. The Admiralty headquarters were in Kinge Street and the brothers Algernon and Robert Sydney, who had many relatives connected with the Admiralty, lived in the street. Lucy knew this, for her mother had told her before leaving Pembrokeshire that she might become acquainted with some of the greatest families in the land. Sighing, she realised her father was not going to take the trouble to introduce her to his friends. To a spirited young girl, eager to taste all the pleasures that London society might afford, the constant company of Marie and Justus could be irksome in the extreme.

As Lucy sat there, feeling increasingly bored, a little dark shape came into view. A scrap of furry kitten miaowed at the window and when Lucy saw her, her heart melted. Leaning out, she scooped the kitten in her arms, burying her face in its soft, fluffy fur, delighting at the feel of its rough tongue against her cheek. Presuming it to have escaped from another attic nearby, Lucy whispered into the ear of the little cat in her arms, 'I am not going to let you go, ever.'

Tiptoeing down the stairs, lest Marie hear her, Lucy made her way to the kitchen. She had been expressly forbidden to go anywhere near the kitchen, and not to mix with the kitchen maids, but she forgot all this now. She needed milk and some fish for the little kitten, who was awaiting her. Pushing open the door, Lucy saw Susan, the scullery maid, cleaning the silver. The girl had a pale face, as though she never saw the sun, and although Lucy judged her to be older than herself, her dress hung loosely on her frame, as though she had no flesh to fill it out.

'Yes, miss?' said the girl enquiringly, bobbing a curtsey.

'Is there some fish left from dinner? A little milk, too, if you have any.' The girl looked baffled at this request, until Lucy explained excitedly to her about the kitten.

'There's milk aplenty, miss, but no fish in the house at all,' replied the girl, wondering what all the fuss was about over a stray kitten. She ladled a saucerful of milk from the churn and gave it to Lucy, who took it thankfully.

'You'll be needing more than sweet milk to feed a kitten, miss. Shall I fetch some crumb bread to break into the milk?' She had a kind heart and soon she had found some soft bread. Looking at Lucy thoughtfully, she said, 'I knows where we could be getting some fish, miss, if you've a mind to it.' Seeing Lucy's interested look, she continued, 'I knows a fishmonger not far from here. He's me uncle, and I could take you there and back in no time.'

Lucy hesitated for only a second before saying she would take the saucer to the kitten and return directly.

'Mind and bring some coins with you,' called the girl. 'You'll not be diddled, though.'

Tying her bonnet with the long pink ribbons firmly onto her head, Lucy felt a thrill of excitement to be out on the London streets, unfettered by Marie, whose restraining presence always made her feel like a child. Ahead of them on the road was a group of Puritan soldiers, Noll Cromwell's men. With their basin haircuts and large, plain white collars, they were not as dashing as the Cavaliers Lucy had become accustomed to in Roch. Susan had a fit of the giggles when she saw them, but a nudge from Lucy quietened her. As the girls passed by, the soldiers turned to bow and Lucy, always mindful of her manners, and wishing to return a pretty compliment, curtsied. Maybe the Puritan soldiers were not as dull as they were made out to be, she thought.

Susan's uncle had a stall not far from Kinge Street, but there was little fish left at that time of day.

'Scraps will do,' said Susan. 'They will suit a lost kitten.'

And so, for one small coin, Lucy was given a parcel of scraps big enough to make a dinner for a poor family.

On the way back, Lucy insisted on stopping at the baker's shop and buying some ginger fairings. She did not see the need to rush and she was enjoying herself. As they ate the biscuits, Susan noticed Lucy's attention drawn to one particular house, where a scantily clad girl sat in the window, her face heavily made up. A procession of men was going in and out of the door.

'Ain't you seen a place like that before?' enquired the maid.

Seeing the mystified look on Lucy's face, the girl giggled.

'It's one of those houses,' and she nudged Lucy, 'you know, where fallen women work.'

Realisation was dawning on Lucy, slowly.

'Maggie was the village whore in Roch, but she did not live in a house like that.'

'She should come to London then, where business is brisk.'

Lucy laughed and popped another biscuit into her mouth.

By the time they arrived home it was late afternoon and Lucy deemed it best for her to go in through the front door, while Susan took the tradesmen's entrance. She was half-way up the stairs when the door of the little parlour opened and Marie appeared at the foot of the stairs. Even in the dim light, Lucy could see she had been crying.

'Lucy, where have you been?' she wailed. You and Justus went missing this afternoon. Oh, you bad, bad pair.'

Ignoring the first part of her question, Lucy said, 'Is Justus not at home?'

'He is now, but neither of you were in your rooms this afternoon when I came to see if you were alright.'

'But you said we would not be going out and I thought I would not be missed if I only went out for a little while.'

'But where have you been?'

'Only to fetch some fish for a starving kitten.'

She knew how to wheedle her way round Marie and

going down the stairs Lucy wrapped her arms around her neck and planted tiny little kisses on her cheeks.

'Now, don't be cross with me, dear Marie, I only wanted fish to feed a little kitten.'

Lucy's charms seemed to be working and Marie's countenance improved. Lucy was a delightful child, but she was not completely satisfied yet.

'Did anything happen to you while you were out?'

'No, of course it didn't, you silly little Marie. I went directly to the fishmonger and stopped only a minute at the baker's on the way back. Look,' she said triumphantly, 'I've saved some fairings for you.'

'Well,' said Marie hesitantly, 'not a word of this escapade to your mother, for I promised her faithfully that no harm would come to you in London town.'

At last, Lucy was able to return to the little kitten in the attic, whom she christened Suki.

News reached London, that summer of 1644, that a decisive Parliamentarian victory had occurred at Marston Moor on July 22nd. Cromwell wrote exultantly to Colonel Valentine Walton of the success of his army, 'God made them as stubble to our swords. Give glory, all the glory, to God.'

Lucy's heart sank when she heard her father discussing it with Marie. Silently, she prayed Richard Palmer was not of the number that fell to the swords of the 'Saints'.

In the late summer, Lucy and Justus returned to Dynefor, and to the care of their mother. Elizabeth Walter marvelled when she saw the changes a season in London had made to her children. Lucy could no longer be mistaken for a child by anyone and Justus, with his deepening voice and soft growth of facial hair, would soon be a man. She felt an overwhelming surge of pride. Her marriage to William Walter had long turned sour, yet two good things had come out of the marriage. She would always be grateful for having Lucy and Justus.

The winter months passed quietly, Lucy taking daily rides

on her pony, Molly, and Suki, the kitten who had now grown into a sleek cat, enjoying her hunting sprees in the surrounding fields.

The winter months gave way to a sparkling green spring. There was great excitement in Dynefor. Richard, Elizabeth's cousin and second Earl of Carbery, was to be honoured by a visit from the King.

Lady Carbery indulged in a frantic burst of housekeeping. The Great Hall was beeswaxed, the floors swept with sweet smelling herbs, all the tapestries were brushed, extra candles with fine cotton wicks made, new pillows conjured with feathers from the poultry yard. Elizabeth Walter enjoyed the hustle and bustle that was going on around her and the activities brightened her spirits, which had been low of late. Richard Vaughan summoned the tailor and commanded him to make new clothes for all the household.

'Mother, does this dress become me?' demanded Lucy one day, prancing around her bedchamber, two bright spots of colour high on her cheekbones. Lucy was clad in a dress of palest lavender silk, a satin sash of blush pink around her small waist. Looking at her daughter, her golden brown ringlets set off by a suntanned complexion, a result of her daily rides, Elizabeth could not help thinking that whatever Lucy might wear could not fail to flatter her. Elizabeth wondered again what sort of marriage match Lucy might make. The Vaughans were highly connected, mixing with the likes of the Earls of Northumberland and Leicester, and families renowned throughout England, like the Sydney and the Percy families, but what match could Lucy hope to make without family money behind her? Elizabeth put these thoughts out of her mind now, to reply to her daughter's question. 'You look lovely, dearest,' she said, and she meant it. Lucy would gladden the heart of any true man, she felt.

And so, on a day so beautiful it seemed heaven and earth had kissed each other, His Majesty, King Charles I, accompanied by his son Charles, the young Prince, arrived at the sweet and plentiful seat of the Vaughans, Earls of Carbery.

At dinner that day, the best silver plate and goblets were set out. The table was laid with salmon from the River Towy, lamb that had fed on grass nurtured by the river water, joints of beef, pork and venison. Game there was in plenty, including pheasants, swans, larks and pigeons. Lucy was so excited to find that she was seated opposite the young Prince that she ate little of the main course but when it came to the desserts she was unable to resist her favourite marchpane. She noticed that the Prince, too, had a sweet tooth.

Observing the Prince shyly from under her fringed, dark ashes, Lucy noted that his mouth was not as finley chiselled as that of Richard Palmer, but his locks, though dark, were equally long and flowing and his black eyes were never serious for long, sparkling with more than a hint of fun in them. Drinking deeply from his goblet, his eyes caught hers and the glance he gave her caused her to blush very deeply.

It was later that evening, when her cousin Carbery sat long with the King, drinking port, that Lucy, making her way to her bedchamber, stopped for a moment to play a tune on the virginal, in one of the side rooms leading from the Great Hall. It was a sad tune, but one she liked well. A haunting refrain, it told of a love that was lost and gone forever. Softly, under her breath, she hummed the tune. To her surprise, she heard a light baritone, humming in unison with her. Assuming it to be Justus behind her, she continued until the song ended. But it was not Justus who clapped at the end and said 'Bravo! A prettier tune I never heard.'

To Lucy's amazement, it was the Prince himself. To cover her consternation, Lucy arose from the seat, and turned and gave the most elegant curtsey she was capable of. Words failed her, but the Prince was equal to the occasion.

'I am pleased to make your acquaintance, Mistress Lucy Walter.'

'How, how did you know my name, Sir?' she enquired.

'Ah! but I made it my business to find out the name of the

charming young lady who so enthralled me when she sat opposite me at dinner!'

Lucy's thoughts were jumbled in her mind. Never for a moment had she allowed herself to believe that the Prince might have noticed her.

Oh, what would Mama say when she told her. Would she think she was telling tall tales about meeting the Prince? But the Prince was bowing now, and making his departure.

'I hope we shall meet again, another time, when you are in London next, perhaps!' and with that he was gone.

In a dream Lucy went to her room. Oh, but the Prince was charming, was handsome, was so polite. Oh! that he should have noticed her and taken the trouble to find out her name. It was all too much to take in in one day. She would go to bed and dream all night about him, and then tomorrow she would think about him again.

Lucy slept late the next day and when she awoke at noon, it was to find that the King, Prince Charles and all the Royal party had already left. Although she felt disappointed, she had so much to remember about the previous night's encounter, that she spent the day in a happy daze, hardly listening to her mother when she spoke to her.

Some weeks after the Royal encounter, news came that the King's men had suffered an overwhelming defeat at Naseby, during the month of June, forcing the King to surrender. Carbery was plunged into gloom. The local news was no better, either. Elizabeth had received a letter from Marie, who was staying in Haverfordwest with her sister. She read it slowly, 'There has been fierce fighting at Colby Moor, just outside Haverfordwest. Many of the King's men have been slain. The battle field was a sodden mess. Those who were there said the place stank to high heaven . . . so many men and horses rotting on the field . . . the men have now been buried in Wiston Church.'

Elizabeth put the letter away and sighed. She had so many problems. Her cousin Carbery had advised her to make speedy recourse to Parliament and present a suit for divorce.

It was the only way William Walter could be forced to provide for his children.

The lawsuit dragged on into the winter of 1646. Elizabeth made a vigorous representation, claiming her husband was disloyal to her bed and had been unfaithful to the marriage vows, with numerous women. Furthermore, he kept a maidservant, by whom he had two children and forced Elizabeth to care for them as though they were her own. Money that she had earned honestly was used to feed and clothe them. It was too much for mortal flesh to bear, but bear it Elizabeth had to, failure or refusal to do so resulting in beatings for her. Elizabeth had no intention of sparing William Walter and further alleged he had numerous other illegitimate children that he was not prepared to acknowledge.

Decision was not made until 1647. Parliament had no reason to disbelieve Eliza Walter's testimony, but it was her fervent support of the Royalist cause and the enthusiasm of her relative Carbery, for the King, that stuck in their throats. William Walter was saved by his Parliamentarian sympathies.

Writing from London, to her mother in Nantyrhebog, Elizabeth poured out her anguish, 'The word of my faithless and treacherous husband has been believed and what I have said has been disregarded. The worst of it is, I am to lose my children. Henceforth, their father is to have charge and control of them. It is said I am too beggared to care for them, which is true. Yet, the whole world must know, he has no regard for what is his own flesh and blood. There is little to comfort me, save that Lucy is now all but a woman and Justo will study to follow the calling of a lawyer, which will necessitate him living in London, anyway. My heart is filled with grief.'

William Walter accepted the care of his children with a bad grace. Marie was to be retained to act as personal maid to Lucy. The night before they left Dynefor, she helped Lucy pack her few belongings. Whispering comfortingly in Lucy's ear, she said, 'Perhaps 'tis all for the best. You may become a fine and grand lady in London, with your own big house, servants to command, big suppers every night.'

Lucy laughed wryly. She was too old to believe Marie's fairy stories any longer, but it would be nice if what Marie said came true. Lady Carbery was spending a few weeks in London during the coming summer and had promised to introduce Lucy to some of her friends. Even if she did not capture 'a great high nobleman', as Marie had said once, she might win the heart of a modest captain-of-the-guard. And there would always be Justo's legal friends to entertain. London suddenly became an inviting prospect.

Before leaving Dynefor, Lucy called for Jeremy Taylor, who had been King Charles's Chaplain, to come to her room. For many years the Countess of Carbery had given him protection from Cromwell's men and he was now Chaplain to the Vaughan family.

Taylor was a gentle man, pious and holy. Looking at Lucy that day, he saw a lovely girl whose beauty, he realised, would be more of a burden than an asset, in the loose times they were living in. He hoped no harm would befall her in London, but his hopes were not high. 'Bless you, my child,' he said, opening the Prayer Book at the beautiful collect for the day. When he had finished reading the lovely prayers, Lucy felt her soul refreshed. Whatever else might happen, she would try very hard to be good.

Lady Carbery was as good as her word and arrived in London not long after Lucy's departure from Golden Grove. Accompanying her were a large retinue of servants, some sides of Welsh smoked ham and boxes and boxes of ball gowns that her dressmaker had made specially for the London season.

'Now, Lucy, you and I are about the same size. You can help yourself to whichever dresses take your eye. Anything that does not fit exactly, Marie can adjust with a few stitches, I'm sure.'

Lucy's eyes gleamed. Why, this was a different London from the one she and Justo had previously inhabited. No more dreary needlework lessons where she pricked her fingers so badly that the blood stained the linen cloth she was working on, no more early nights and long hours of boredom in between. No, this was a London where people entertained their highly placed friends to vast suppers followed by musical entertainments.

The Vaughan family had a town house in the Saint Giles area and Lady Carbery meant to make the most of the winter season. Life could be very humdrum in Dynefor. She planned to give great suppers, followed by music and dancing, each week. Lucy Walter, her husband's young kinswoman was sure to be a big attraction at these events. Lady Carbery was very fond of Lucy and she meant to launch her in London society, since her poor mother was not able to and her father was unwilling to. If Lucy did not find a match by the end of the season, then it would not be through lack of effort on Lady Carbery's part.

'Lucy, I want you to look very special,' said Lady Carbery, for she was of a generous nature and in no way was she jealous of Lucy.

'Try this gown on. I think it would look very becoming on you and your colouring would show it off beautifully.'

She held out a dress of white figured satin, a lace petticoat peeping out from underneath.

'Look, there are slippers to go with it, and this velvet cloak which has a fur trim.'

Lucy could hardly speak, the excitement was getting too much for her. Could all this really be happening to her, Lucy Walter, who had had to manage on her mother's hand-me-downs for years?

The gown fitted beautifully, the folds of material shining softly in the candle-lit boudoir.

'There,' said Lady Carbery, delightedly clapping her hands.

'You like it and it suits you beautifully. This very week we shall see you in it, for I have arranged a supper for Friday night.'

Lucy was overwhelmed by the generosity of her relative, but it was so typical of her. She could hardly wait for Friday night to come.

When Lucy told Marie about the gown and the supper, the old nurse, who now also acted as her chaperone, was almost as excited as Lucy. They began to make their preparations in earnest.

'We will go round to the Vaughan's house in the early afternoon. I shall bath you and wash your hair and bind it tightly in rags. You shall rest a while then, to be fresh for the evening, when I shall dress you in your lovely new clothes.' Marie was determined Lucy would look her best. As Lucy prattled on, the stars shining in her eyes, Marie was glad that things seemed to be working out well now that the Lady Carbery had taken Lucy under her wing. Perhaps good might well come out of all this trouble, after all.

At last Friday came. A fire had been lit in one of the dressing rooms of the large Vaughan house. By the time Marie had filled a large wooden tub with hot water and scattered sweet smelling herbs in it, not a trace of chilliness remained. After Lucy had bathed, Marie rubbed her hair dry in front of the blazing fire. She dressed Lucy in her nightdress, then tucked her up in the day bed with a warm glass of posset. After that Lucy dozed until it was time to have her hair dressed.

'It is not hard to make you look beautiful, my lady,' said Marie, standing back to survey Lucy. 'But there, there is no need for me to tell you that, for there'll be plenty of young men present tonight who will let you know.' Her eyes twinkled. She loved grand, social occasions.

'Do I really look lovely, Marie?' Lucy was not a vain girl and rarely before had she had the chance to parade herself in this way.

Lucy was like her own flesh and blood to Marie, and if Lucy wanted reassurance, she was only too pleased to be able to give it to her.

'Your mother would be very proud of you, if she could

see you now.' This brought a wistful look into Lucy's eyes, so Marie decided that she had better not mention Elizabeth Walter too often, for fear it made Lucy sad.

Just then, there was a tap on the door. Marie answered.

'Please, but my Lady Carbery wishes to see Mistress Lucy in her Ladyship's dressing room.'

'I'll go now, Marie. I'll not be gone long.'

On seeing Lucy, Lady Carbery's face broke into a smile. She kissed the girl warmly on the cheek. She was indeed a beauty and the gown flattered her tawny colouring, throwing into relief the high colour of her complexion, the rich burgundy sheen of her hair, the lustrousness of her eyes.

'There is only one thing lacking in your attire, my dear,' she said, her eyes twinkling.

'Yes, Ma'am?' Lucy said, uncertainly.

For answer, Lady Carbery went to a small drawer in her writing table and removed a blue velvet-covered box. Opening it, she held up a necklace of tiny diamonds that caught the light and split it into a million scintillating facets.

'Come here, child,' she commanded. 'This necklace was a gift from my mother, when I made my social debut, when I was about the age you are now. I want you to have this trinket as a present from me. I hope it will give you the same pleasure it gave me.'

Lucy gasped in astonishment. It was so beautiful and she had never owned anything as lovely.

'This is so kind of you,' she murmured, her eyes wide, unable to take in the beauty of the gift, the generosity of her benefactress. 'I hardly know what to say.'

'No need to say anything,' said Lady Carbery, deftly fastening the necklace round Lucy's throat. Just wear the necklace and enjoy it,' and she gave Lucy's cheek a playful tweak.

Lady Carbery certainly knew how to entertain, thought Lucy later that evening, surveying the crowded table. Mutton, pork, beef, venison, there was, to be sure, but the surprise of the evening was yet to come.

'Aha! Here comes the cook with a very great plate,' said Lucy's partner at the dining table. She had been placed next to Lord Glamorgan, a close friend of John Barlow of Slebech, Lucy's cousin. Lucy had not met him before, but judged that the distinguished looking man at her side must have been in his early forties. While she was silently contemplating him, the cook carefully cut the pie-crust and, amazingly, out jumped twenty live frogs, or maybe more. The cries and shrieks of the ladies filled the air, but Lucy sat serenely through it all. Taking her hand in his, Lord Glamorgan turned to his young companion, impressed with her dignity: 'I see you are a true country girl at heart. It would take more than a few frogs to shake your composure, I'm sure.'

Lucy smiled. He had nice teeth and kind eyes. If he had not been so much older than her, he was the type of man she could have grown to like. Lady Carbery had explained to her earlier that she would have liked to place her next to someone more her own age, but as she had only just arrived in London, and with so many young men away on the King's cause, Lord Glamorgan was the best she could manage that night. Besides, he had many good contacts and might be useful to them in other ways.

It was a full quarter of an hour before the merriment subsided and the diners were able to continue. Further culinary delights were to follow, and they were regaled with fish, snipe, larks and carbonadoes, as much as they could eat, and more.

When it was time for the sweet course, Lucy's companion, Lord Glamorgan prevailed upon her to try a little of the sugar sops, for, he said, 'It is very good.'

'Oh, really,' laughed Lucy, 'what is a girl to do when she is encouraged to eat all this beautiful food. I really should not, your Lordship, or I shall surely burst the seams of my gown.'

Glamorgan may have been in the middling years of his life, but he had not yet reached that age when the charms of a pretty woman were no longer of any consequence to him. Casting an eye over Lucy's trim figure, he observed, 'A little more weight could only add to your beauty, Madam.'

He was such a chivalrous gentleman and Lucy found him a most agreeable companion, despite the disparity in their ages. Later, when they danced together, she allowed him to flirt a little with her, much to his Lordship's delight. He, on his part, found it most gratifying that he could still make a young girl's eyes sparkle.

Lucy spent the next day in a dream. She had enjoyed herself so much and Lady Carbery told her, before she had left the previous evening, that there would be many more entertainments. Therefore, it came as a shock to receive a note from her kinswoman, informng her that Lady Carbery's mother had been taken ill, and that Frances Carbery had been obliged to return to Wales with all haste to care for her. With Lady Carbery's departure Lucy could see only months of tedium in London lying ahead of her.

A few days later, to Lucy's surprise, a messenger came to Kinge Street, bearing an invitation. Lucy, Justo and their father were graciously invited by the Earl and Countess of Leicester to sup at their London house on the Wednesday of that week. Lucy had been unaware that her father was acquainted with the family and on enquiring of William Walter how well he knew the Leicesters, he replied, 'The Countess of Leicester, Lady Dorothy, is a kinswoman of your cousin, John Barlow, of Slebech. I have made their acquaintance during the years I have been in London. I find the whole family most agreeable and, of course, they are of the Parliamentarian persuasion.'

Lucy had no great interest in politics. The second part of the Civil War was raging across the country, but all she could think of was poor King Charles, a prisoner at Carisbrooke Castle. He had looked so happy that time she had seen him in Golden Grove, with his son, Prince Charles.

Still, there was nothing she could do about the unrest in the country so, instead, she turned her mind to the Leicesters' invitation. Marie was most impressed when Lucy told her; she had always known the Walter family to have good connections.

'It will have to be the same gown I wore the other evening at Lady Carbery's, for I have no other and no means to buy another, either,' said Lucy ruefully.

'I'll put a hot iron over it and you will look just as beautiful as you did last week,' said the faithful servant.

Arriving at the Leicester's house, they were shown into the large hall, which had a long table running down the middle, laden with food. Lucy became aware of a tall, dark man staring openly at her. In the candlelight, Lucy's skin gleamed like marble and she had an incandescence about her that those who came into contact with her could not fail to notice. Lucy did not know that the man whose attention she had captured was Algernon Sydney, a colonel in Cromwell's army of 'Saints', like his brother Robert. But William Walter had not missed that look of open admiration that Lucy had been given and it occurred to him then that even a girl without a dowry was capable of catching a rich husband if she had the looks, and Lucy did.

Algernon Sydney strode across the room and bowed low to the Walter family. He had met William Walter on previous occasions and felt tonight what he had felt previously for him, and that was indifference. Only this very day he had heard the fellow was complaining to Parliament that he was being asked to pay tax on the money he had been granted by the House of Lords. Why, the fellow was beyond contempt. But his daughter was another matter, another matter altogether. William Walter was equal to the occasion, sensing the man's interest in his daughter.

'May I present my family, Sir? This is my son Justus, and my daughter Lucy.'

Algernon Sydney gave Justus scant attention, but his eyes lingered over Lucy. Holding out his arm, he asked, 'May I escort you to supper, Madam?'

Sitting next to Colonel Algernon Sydney during the

meal, Lucy discovered that, though the man might not have good looks to recommend him, indeed might even be considered ugly by some, his manners were impeccable and he treated her most courteously.

'Have you been in London long, Mistress Lucy?' he enquired.

'Only a short while, Sir, and I was enjoying myself until my cousin's wife, Lady Carbery, had need to return to Dynefor.'

On hearing Lucy's account of events, leading up to Lady Carbery's return to Llandeilo, Sydney's face grew serious.

'Your father supports our cause, I understand.'

'Yes, Sir, that is true.'

'But Lady Carbery is an affirmed Royalist?'

'The Carberys support His Majesty, the King.'

'And you lived in Roch previously, which is close to West Haverford?'

'Yes, Sir, that is correct.'

Sydney sat back in his chair for a moment, wondering how much he should tell his companion.

'Oliver Cromwell has been entertained at Golden Grove by Lady Carbery, since her return from London.' He paused to allow his companion to absorb what he was saying. Hearing Lucy gasp, he patted her hand and continued, 'Do not alarm yourself. You need have no worries on account of Lady Carbery. Richard Vaughan, I regret to say, had prior intelligence of the visit and escaped. Lady Carbery refused to leave her ailing mother.'

Seeing Lucy's face visibly pale, Sydney was sensible to her thoughts.

'No harm has come to Lady Carbery or the estate. Indeed, Lady Carbery proved to be a most gracious hostess and charmed the General.'

At this last remark, he allowed himself a little smile.

Lucy marvelled at the presence of mind Lady Carbery had shown under what must have been very trying conditions. Another, less noble, thought went through her mind. If Lady Carbery did not return to London, and there seemed little possibility of it now, then she was going to be stranded in the house in Kinge Street with no friends, no social contacts and no money. The thought appalled her.

Sydney was a shrewd judge of character and he watched the girl silently for a few moments, before saying softly, 'And where does that leave you, Lucy Walter?'

Lucy's face flushed. Was her predicament so patently obvious, even to a complete stranger like Algernon Sydney?

'Think about it,' he said, in a low voice.

They had finished their meal and in an adjoining room a fiddler was scraping a tune. Couples were leaving the table and drifting towards the music. Rising from the table, he helped her from her chair.

'And while you are thinking about it, perhaps you would care to accompany me to the library?'

Taking her arm, he led her out through a side door, till they reached the sanctuary of the book-lined room.

Drawing up two chairs, he turned to face her.

'Sit down,' he said commandingly.

'Consider carefully what I have to say to you. I am going to make you an offer, which you are quite at liberty to reject. You may not like what I propose, but I doubt you will get a better deal than the one I am going to propose, your father's finances being in the state they are.'

She was stung by this last remark, and though she knew it to be true, felt duty bound to defend the honour of her father.

'I do not know what you know about my father's finances, Sir, but my father is a gentleman.'

He was nonplussed by this outburst and quietly let her finish before answering.

'Your father a gentleman?' he said, tossing back his head and openly laughing.

'More like a rogue done up in gentleman's clothing, my dear. I cannot think why my mother even bothered to invite your family here this evening.'

His voice softened, 'Though I am very glad she did, because otherwise I would not have met you.' Taking her hand, he kissed it slowly, then his eyes met hers and he said, 'Sweet Lucy,' and it was said with tenderness.

'Come, let us not have harsh words between us. I will only say this more about your father and you would be wise to listen to me. It is well known in the city that William Walter is next door to being a beggar. Now, what do you say to that?'

He had spoken the truth and there was little that Lucy could say. Silently, she had to concede victory to the proud man sitting at her side. In her heart Lucy knew William Walter had no time for her and Justo. Even if he had money, were the circumstances different, Lucy doubted she and Justus would see any of it.

'What is your proposal?' she asked in a quiet voice, realising she had no bargaining power.

'My proposal,' he said slowly, 'is that I give you fifty broad pieces, to do with as you will — buy yourself some fine clothes, or anything else you may deem necessary. I do not want it said that Algernon Sydney does not treat his mistress generously.'

Lucy was stunned into silence for a moment. She was a young girl who had spent most of her life in the country, yet she understood that what he was offering her had its advantages. In return for money, he would own her body. It was as simple as that. Marriage would have been more respectable and secure, of course, but under the circumstances perhaps she would be wise not to refuse him. It might be the best offer she would get in a long time.

Looking him straight in the eyes, she said, 'I accept your proposal.'

'I thought you might. You are a wise girl.'

His voice took on a softer tone, 'Come to me, little one. I shall see that you do not regret your bargain.'

He pulled her to her feet and kissed her firmly, even roughly, on the mouth. He was not as gentle as Richard

Palmer had been, but neither was she the innocent girl who had walked through the heather all those years ago with the dashing baronet. That had all been a long time ago and she knew a little more of the ways of the world by now.

Striding over to the wall, Algernon Sydney removed a wooden panel, to reveal a hidden safe. Opening the safe door, he reached inside and removed a heavy leather purse. He shut the safe door and replaced the panel carefully. Turning to Lucy, he handed her the money.

'Should there be any trouble from your father, which I very much doubt, I shall shut his mouth easily enough with a few gold coins, I daresay.'

He looked at Lucy, who appeared about to say something, but no words were uttered, and he concluded that she was beginning to learn what was best for her, if she wished to survive in what was most definitely a hostile world for a penniless young girl.

In the days that followed, if Lucy had any doubts about the wisdom of the agreement she had entered into with Algernon Sydney, she did not allow them to prevent her from going on a wild spending spree.

'Look, Marie, did you ever see a lovelier dress than this?'

Lucy twirled across the floor in a rosebud patterned muslin gown, with a big bow at the back. 'Does it become me?'

Marie smiled indulgently. It was a mystery to her where the money had come from for Mistress Lucy's new clothes but, goodness, she had needed them. Perhaps William Walter was not as mean a man as she had taken him to be.

That morning Lucy had received a communication from Colonel Sydney, telling her that soon he would be setting her up in a little house in Chiswick. She would have a housekeeper and a maid to do her bidding. Whenever he was in London, he would call on her in Chiswick. Reading the letter again, Lucy thought the prospect seemed delightful. 'Prince Charles is in Holland,' wrote Sydney, 'and things are quiet in the country at the moment, so I see no reason why you and I cannot spend some time together before my regiment needs me.'

The following evening Justus tapped on Lucy's door. His studies for the Bar kept him busy and Lucy did not see as much of him as she would have liked to.

'Come, let's drink a goblet or two,' he said, brandishing a bottle of brandy.

Settling themselves in comfortable chairs, Lucy was surprised when Justo began speaking about the man who had been occupying so many of her thoughts lately.

'Lucy, you remember Algernon Sydney, the man who took such an interest in you when we were at the Leicesters the other night?'

Lucy nodded guardedly that she did.

'I was speaking to his brother Henry when I was on my way to the Middle Temple today. Henry is not a soldier like the other two. He was saying that Algernon and Robert had been called to Haverford today. It was all very unexpected and they left in great haste.'

Mistaking the flush on Lucy's cheeks for concern for the old town they knew so well, Justus continued, 'The news is not good, I fear, not good at all. Cromwell has garrisoned the town and ordered the destruction of the castle. To ensure his orders are carried out, he has sent for more troops. He is very thorough in all he does.'

Affecting a tone of disinterest, Lucy asked, 'How long are the troops expected to be away?'

'No-one really knows,' said Justus, unaware of the impact his news had made upon his sister. 'Do not trouble yourself about Harford; things may not be as bad as we think, but it is as well we are away from the unrest.'

After Justus's departure, Lucy sat far into the night wondering what was to become of the bargain between the Puritan Colonel and herself. He might not live to claim his share; if he did not return alive she would shed no tears, for she had received her fifty broad pieces.

Chapter 4

The English Channel was choppy, but the company of the Herberts and their Royalist friends helped make it a tolerable crossing for Lucy. Now that she was finally on her way to Holland, she had no regrets about leaving behind her life in London. A girl from an impoverished family had little chance of making a good match in London town and Lucy had heard that on the Continent society was not so rigidly class bound. She gave a little sigh, audible only to herself, for she had learnt it was as well to hide one's feelings when one could not afford to express them. She was here in her official capacity as companion to Lady Herbert, and she was sure that particular lady did not want the company of a miserable young woman. Whether or not she would be successful in finding a rich man, only time would tell.

On reaching The Hague, Lord Herbert escorted his party to a tall, gracious town house he had secured for them, overlooking a canal and fronting a pretty square. Lucy marvelled at the blueness of the sky, the quaintness of the cobbled streets and the air of sparkling freshness that everything she came into contact with in Holland seemed to have. Oh! she was sure she was going to enjoy her stay in the Netherlands.

A meal had been prepared for them by the Dutch housekeeper, whose services Lord Herbert had secured. She came with the highest references, and if the meal she had cooked for them was anything to go by, they were going to be well satisfied.

'We will not unpack any more than we need for the night, my dear,' said Lady Herbert. 'You are tired after the arduous journey and voyage we have had. Tomorrow Anneka, the housekeepers's niece, will come to help you.'

Alone in her room, Lucy reflected on the kindness of the Herberts. She saw no reason why she should not be happy with them.

A fire sparkled in the grate and the blankets of the bed had been turned back, ready for the night. A pitcher of hot water stood on the washstand and Lucy was glad to wash and change out of her travelling clothes.

After breakfast the following day, Lady Herbert summoned Lucy to her private sitting room.

'I hope you are refreshed and have slept well?' she enquired.

'I slept very well, thank you, ma'am.'

'Good. Now, I would like to discuss with you some of the things I am planning in the way of entertainment during the following weeks. I think the sooner we invite friends and acquaintances to visit us, the sooner our social calendar will be filled. We must let all our English friends in The Hague know that we have arrived safely, so what better way to do it than to issue invitations?' She laughed delightedly at her own idea. Looking at her in the morning light, Lucy saw a woman in early middle age, still retaining the vivacity and vigour of youth. Her fine skin, wrinkling lightly around her eyes and mouth, still retained a translucency, and her periwinkle blue eyes were typically English. She had been a great beauty, and still retained a handsomeness that time could not deny.

'Can you keep a secret?'

Lucy nodded.

'Well, I am going to ask Prince Charles to supper and an entertainment in this house, soon.' She paused, and looked at Lucy closely.

'That surprised you, didn't it?' she said triumphantly, clapping her hands girlishly. 'Oh, we're going to have a marvellous time. You see, the exiled court is largely on the Continent, in Holland, at the moment. My husband, in his youth, served King Charles in the Royal Household. The Crown Prince often went riding with Lord Herbert, who was a very skilled horseman. Lord Herbert taught the Prince a great deal about horsemanship and that is why the Prince is such a fine rider now,' she said, with pride. 'I do not expect Prince Charles to refuse our invitation. Indeed, I'm sure he will only be too delighted to join us.'

'When are you planning to hold the supper?' enquired Lucy.

'Oh, some time towards the end of the next week. We must allow time to issue the invitations and receive the replies, of course, and the menu must be planned carefully. What I want you to do today is unpack my clothes. Inspect your dresses and choose one that will suit the occasion when the Prince comes. If you have nothing suitable, then there is time to have one made. Anneka will help you, and I have engaged her permanently as my personal maid. See that Anneka presses and airs my lavender gown, as I've a mind to wear it when the Prince comes.'

'Yes, ma'am,' said Lucy dutifully, turning to go.

'And one other thing, Lucy. You see that you get forty winks during the day, then you and I will take a carriage ride through The Hague before tea. I mean to see all the sights!'

As Lucy deftly unpacked her mistress's beautiful clothes, she reflected on the prospect of having the Prince as a guest under their roof. How attentive and charming he had been all those years ago at Golden Grove. He would not remember the girl with the brown curls and the rosy cheeks who played a haunting tune on the virginal, but she had never forgotten him. What woman would, or could, she thought, seeing again his dark, swarthy looks, the soulful eyes that held a depth of understanding. Yes, he was truly a King's son, destined to be a King himself, when time and the hour called him. Displaying all the confidence of his Royal heritage, he still retained an appealing meekness that allowed for no arrogance in his personality. Only the same age as herself, he had appeared a man of the world, at ease in whatever company he found himself. All Lucy would be able to do would be to dream of him, she realised, for he would never spare her a second glance. In fact, it had been whispered on the crossing, Charles had fallen a little in love with Margaret de Carteret, kinswoman of the governor of the island of Jersey, whom he had met when the exiles sought refuge there, but it was known that Henrietta Maria, the Prince's mother, had set her heart on his marrying 'La Grande Mademoiselle' herself, Anne-Marie-Louise, daughter of Gaston, Duc d'Orleans, and the richest heiress in the whole of Europe. Well, whoever he married, she hoped it would be a true love match, for a man so gay, so kind, deserved nothing less.

To be in Holland with the exiled court was more than Lucy would have ever dreamed possible when she had been little more than a child in Roch and had passed the tedious winter months wondering if another type of life might exist far away from Pembrokeshire. She never wanted to be back in her father's draughty castle or dreary house in Covent Garden.

Lucy understood enough about frugal living to have saved a hefty portion of the money given to her by Algernon Sydney. She had taken it to buy her freedom from that half-life her father provided, and now the knowledge that it was always there if she had dire need of it, gave her a certain sense of security which she found liberating.

There were those who would have said that in accepting Sydney's money, Lucy had made a moral choice, which would set in motion its own repercussions. Others, of a more charitable nature, would have said that for a penniless young woman, there had been no choice. Lucy, if she had been aware of the debate, would have agreed with the latter.

Lucy lived the next few days in a state of pleasurable

anticipation. She could not wait to see the Prince again, to be in the same room as him, breathing the same air. Perhaps she was nothing but a foolish young girl, but she did like to be in the presence of handsome men, especially when one of them had the advantage of being royal, a charmer and heir to the English throne!

The rose-sprigged muslin dress hung on the back of a chair. It had been worn on a previous occasion, but it retained a new, fresh appearance. Lucy held the dress in front of her. It would suit her as well as any and, besides, the roses in the dress echoed the roses in her cheeks, lending a country dewiness that was noticeably lacking in many society ladies.

That evening, before getting ready herself, Lucy helped Lady Herbert to dress her hair with glittering combs and hang diamond hoops from her ears. Although Georgina Herbert was known for her sparkling wit and ready repartee, there was a thoughtful and serious side to her nature, and as she sat quietly enjoying Lucy's attentions, she puzzled about the competent girl, from the wilds of Wales, who was attending her.

The Herberts had known very little about Lucy when they had accepted her into their household, yet she had fitted in very well with their way of life. Lord Glamorgan had vouched for her honesty and integrity, but beyond saying that engaging Lucy as a companion to her ladyship would almost be an act of charity, they were told little else about her background. Certainly, Georgina Herbert had no complaints against Lucy and enjoyed her presence, having no daughters of her own.

Watching Lucy put out her satin shoes, Lady Herbert noted Lucy's white hands, soft as a milkmaid's, the rounded innocence of her face, the meekness of her manner, and felt all the more perplexed about that part of her that was disturbing and wholly unchildlike. There were missing parts to this puzzle, and the knowledge that she came from a good family did nothing to dispel her misgivings. Undoubtedly,

Lucy was used to mixing with the gentry, but equally she knew her place as a companion and could fade into the background when necessary. She sighed. For the moment, she was unable to solve this conundrum. Best to push aside these uneasy feelings and take the girl at face value. Whatever, she was a great help and tonight Georgina Herbert was determined that Lucy would enjoy herself.

The Herberts were lavish hosts and, at very short notice, had prepared a veritable feast for the Crown Prince and his retinue. Lucy's interest in the food, however, was minimal. Her eyes sparkled like diamonds and she radiated a luminosity which commanded the attention of all those present. All heads turned in her direction as she entered the dining room on the arm of Lord Herbert's major domo. There was not one man in that room whose heart did not leap at the beauty of the young girl from an unknown place in Wales.

Charles Stuart took his seat as guest of honour at the head of the dining table, his host at his side. Once he was settled in his chair, he let his gaze rest on Lucy.

'I see Mistress Lucy has caught your attention, Your Highness,' remarked Lord Herbert.

Charles's eyes lingered on Lucy, and he fingered his beard thoughtfully. 'That face stirs some memory in me, yet I cannot recall where I have seen it before, or whether or not it is a face that came to me only in my dreams.'

Lord Herbert chuckled quietly. For a man so young, Charles was very appreciative of lovely women.

'I see you have a poetic turn of phrase, Sir. I will admit that Lucy looks like an angel, but she is truly flesh and blood, and is kith and kin to the Carbery family of Dynefor, Sire, ever your loyal supporters, I am reliably informed.'

'Ah! It all becomes clear to me now. I must have met her at Golden Grove when I visited that delightful place with the King, my dear father, some years ago.'

The soup was served and the Prince turned his attention

to the food, the conversation and the gossip from England that the new arrivals brought.

Under her lowered eyelashes, Lucy watched the future King of England holding court with those around him, as much at ease as though he had been at home in Saint James's Palace. Charles Stuart was every bit as handsome as she had remembered him in Golden Grove. His presence stirred up memories of the happy times she had enjoyed at Dynefor. Charles had not lost the gaiety he had displayed then and a life of forced wanderings and narrow escapes had honed his boyish features into a manliness he had not formerly possessed. Lucy thought wistfully how she could have given her heart to such a man, but future kings married princesses, not such as she.

The evening sped by, given impetus by the air of celebration that hung over the proceedings. Soon it was time for the Prince to take his leave of that loyal gathering. As he made his departure, he noticed Lucy, paused and, with a flourish, made a low bow to her and then was gone, disappearing out into the night air.

'Well, my dear, you certainly made an impression on Prince Charles tonight. Indeed, he remembered you from Golden Grove. The point is,' said Lord Herbert with a twinkle in his eye, 'do you remember him?'

'I could never forget meeting His Royal Highness,' said Lucy, in her soft, quiet voice.

'I will always remember his visit to Cousin Richard's house in Llandeilo. It gave me great joy to see the Prince here tonight.'

'Well spoken, my dear. You are a true friend of the Prince, like myself.'

Lord and Lady Herbert had been invited to a wedding in the country, Georgina Herbert informed Lucy the next day.

'I have arranged for Lady Llewellyn's companion to stay here for a while to keep you company.'

'There really is no need, my lady,' said Lucy. 'I am perfectly able to occupy myself while you are away.'

'I know that, Lucy, but it will be so dull for you with the other servants, for their English is so limited. Besides, Shelagh Macpherson, although older than you, should be quite entertaining. She was governess to Lady Llewellyn's children and has travelled all over the world with them.'

Lucy began to protest again that she would be quite happy with her own company, but Lady Herbert was adamant.

'Not another word about not minding being on your own. I have made all the arrangements and, besides, I shall be happier knowing you will have this sensible woman to turn to if anything goes wrong.'

After the Herberts' carriage had creaked down the road, Lucy began to look forward to the arrival of Shelagh Macpherson. At least, it woud be someone to talk to and she might bring news of London.

It was towards the middle of the afternoon when the Scots woman arrived, clad in heavy tweeds and wearing stout shoes on her feet. Lucy's first impression of her was of a grim, austere person. The other woman spoke first.

'I'm Shelagh Macpherson,' she introduced herself, and you are Lucy Walter?'

Lucy extended her hand and murmured a greeting. Shelagh Macpherson swept a disdainful glance over Lucy's frilly dress with its lace trimmings, bows and frills. There was nothing in the least feminine in the appearance of Lady Llewellyn's companion and Lucy's heart sank. The woman spoke like the governess she had been and Lucy took an immediate dislike to her. When the visitor had gone to unpack her bags, Lucy heaved a sigh, then went to prepare a tea-tray for them. In an effort to comfort herself, she clung to the thought that appearances could be deceptive and they might get along well after a while.

When they had finished tea, the lady's companion brought out some fine needlework.

'Do you sew?' she asked Lucy.

'Not for pleasure, but I can mend clothes quite well.'

'I see,' said the woman, obviously not very impressed with Lucy's reply.

Lucy began to think she would have been better off on her own during Lady Herbert's absence; then she would not have had the tedium of having to sit for endless hours watching someone else sewing.

'Would you like to hear me play a tune on the virginal?' volunteered Lucy.

'Let us hear you then, for I am fond of music,' replied the other woman.

Lucy was a skilled player and the woman sat back and seemed to enjoy listening. After Lucy had been playing a while, Shelagh Macpherson stood up.

'It is my turn now, you have a rest.'

The Scotswoman was a fine player and went easily through a repertoire of songs, singing the words melodiously under her breath. Abruptly, she stopped and said, 'I'll play some melodies for dancing to, now.'

She swung into the Spanish pavane, the Italian pasamezzo and the Branle. Suddenly, she stopped and looked at Lucy. There was something in the look that disturbed Lucy, but she did not know why.

'Do you dance?' asked Shelagh Macpherson.

'When I was in London, with Lady Carbery, I learnt some simple dance steps.'

'Can you dance the pavane?'

'I did not learn that dance.'

'Come,' said the older woman, imperiously. 'I will show you.'

Taking Lucy by the hand, she led her masterfully into the opening steps of the dance. As they twirled, Lucy's lace fichu caught on the woman's brooch, exposing Lucy's breast and a long scratch where the pin's head had caught her. Shelagh Macpherson stopped and looked down.

'I am sorry,' she said and went to free the brooch from the material.

When the pin was free, Lucy went to rearrange her

clothing, but the other woman caught her hand, saying, softly, 'Wait. You have hurt yourself. That scratch must be bathed.'

'No, it's nothing,' Lucy replied.

'Let me see,' said the woman.

Lucy was beginning to find her attention annoying and worrying, but was unsure how to react without appearing rude. The woman ran her fingers over the scratch.

'Yes, perhaps you are right. It needs no further attention.'

Instead of removing her hand, she scooped Lucy's breast in one hand and encircled Lucy's nipple with her finger, saying, 'You really are as beautiful as I was told.'

Macpherson's mouth was coming closer to Lucy's now, but it was too much for Lucy to bear. Trembling, Lucy gathered all her strength and ran from the room, sobs choking and catching in her throat. In her room, she slammed the door and pushed the heavy linen press against it. She threw herself onto the bed, revulsion and horror sweeping over her. After what appeared to be many hours she tiptoed to the washstand and splashed herself with cold water. She felt unclean and all because of that woman, whom she had never seen until that day. Lucy did not blame Georgina Herbert, who could not possibly have known the predilections of Lady Llewellyn's maid. Lucy could only assume that in the past, Shelagh Macpherson had been very careful not to reveal her true nature to her employer. At last, sleep came to her, but she awoke feeling dispirited.

When Lucy went down to breakfast she found a note by her plate, from the woman who had haunted her dreams the previous night. It read, 'I am sorry to have to curtail my visit, but due to an attack of vertigo, I thought it best to get back to familiar surroundings.'

It was signed 'Shelagh Macpherson'.

Lucy crumpled it up in her hand and threw it onto the fire. With a sense of relief, she watched the blue smoke from the paper disappearing up the chimney. Perhaps she had led a very sheltered life, but the sooner she forgot the whole incident the better, she decided.

After Georgina Herbert's return, she wished Lucy to escort her around the medieval streets of The Hague. After the grime of London, everything in Holland seemed freshly washed, but the sight-seeing trip was wasted on Lucy, for since meeting the Prince again she felt a certan dissatisfaction had fallen on her life and she could not quite explain it or even understand it.

'You must get out and about more, my dear,' said her employer, sensing an unaccustomed listlessness in Lucy's demeanour. Lucy did not reply. So much had happened to her, so quickly, during the previous months — the offer of a position as lady's companion, the move to Holland, the dazzling reception for the Prince and now everything seemed to have fallen flat. Many of her days consisted of little more than reading boring tracts of the Bible to Lady Herbert and going for walks in leafy squares. To a young, adventurous girl, this sort of life could never be enough and Lucy was beginning to find her life more than a little boring.

Sensing Lucy's listlessness, Georgina Herbert spoke, 'I know you must find the type of life we lead rather quiet. What you need is to meet more people and have some fun. I promised you that we would lead a busy social life, and so far it has not come about. I have had an invitation from a kinsman to attend a small gathering he is arranging for next week. I was about to reply in the negative, for he is not of the same political persuasion as ourselves.'

She lowered her voice and arched her fine eyebrows: 'He is a Parliamentarian.' Watching Lucy's reaction closely, she continued: 'He has invited us to join him for a quiet meal — just a few carefully selected friends and, as he is family, I think it would be permissible for us to go. It would do you good, and I can let my mother know I have seen her nephew.'

And so it was, a few nights later, that Lucy, dressed in a grey watered silk gown, with extravagant lace trimming, given to her by Lady Herbert, examined her reflection in the glass. The dress might have been considered a little too old for a young girl, but it enhanced Lucy's girlishness, perfectly complementing the naturally high colour of her cheeks.

On arrival, their host greeted the Herberts warmly, then waited to have Lucy presented to him.

'May I introduce Mistress Lucy Walter?' she heard Granville Herbert say, then her outstretched hand was taken in a firm grip and she was aware of a heavily built man, tall above the average, with a heavy chin and dark, prominent eyebrows. The profile of his face was less than handsome, yet Lucy had to admit to herself that here was a man of compelling appearance. To have called him good-looking would have been a distortion of the facts, but there was something about this man that went deeper than outward appearances.

It was towards the middle of the evening, when the dancing was well under way, that Lucy found herself being invited to dance by Robert Sydney. Dark eyes looked enquiringly at her, issuing a challenge. Holding his gaze, she felt his eyes mocking her. It was a challenge she could not resist. Boldly, she stared back at him, accepting.

Strong arms went around her and she felt herself being held a little closer than was necessary. Moving in unison, they partnered each other as though this was not the first time they had danced together. Before the music stopped, he led her to a balcony overlooking a canal. A cold breeze blew off the water and she shivered slightly.

'Here. This will warm you,' he said, pouring each of them a glass of fine, French brandy. As her eyes met his in thanks, Lucy felt again that his glance was too familiar, and she was annoyed that he stared so openly at her. His words, when he spoke, took her off her guard.

'You do not like me looking at you so openly, do you? You are annoyed that my eyes have scarcely left your face all evening.'

It was as though he had read her thoughts. She flushed, cross with herself and him.

'At last I have met the lovely Lucy Walter, whom my brother Algernon thought was his, until he put duty to his country before his own pleasure.'

Slowly, realisation was dawning on Lucy. She was stunned by his words.

'Algernon Sydney?' she whispered.

'Aye, the very same. Algernon Sydney,' he repeated, grasping her roughly to him. Seeing her distress, his grip tightened on her.

'Don't play the innocent with me, my lovely one, for I am not fooled by your pretty ways.'

Putting a finger beneath her chin, he forced her face upwards, then brought his hard mouth down on hers. Lucy was too surprised and shocked to protest. She felt his cold lips, dry and hard, on her own. He was too strong for her to push away. Instinct came to her rescue and, using her sharp, strong teeth, she bit him sharply, till he yelped in pain, letting out a low curse. She pushed him then, catching him off balance, and he reeled backwards against a wall. Wiping his mouth on a linen handkerchief, he laughed.

'Well, I'll say this for you, Lucy Walter, you're a spirited wench.'

Her voice was level and low when she spoke, betraying no sign of anger.

'So, you think that because your brother gave me a gold purse, you have some claim over me?'

Lucy could see that her frankness surprised him, and this gave her courage.

'Well, let me tell you this, whatever bargain existed between your brother and myself, did not include you.'

Turning on her heel, she swiftly walked away.

Watching her retreating back, Sydney felt distinctly pleased with what he had seen of Lucy Walter. It was his philosophy never to buy a pig in a poke. He applied this homily to his every day affairs. So far, it had stood him in good stead.

Spirited and beautiful, it was true that she had rebuffed him, but he knew that a shortage of money tempted people down paths that they would never have dreamt of taking, if circumstances had not forced them. His brother had supplied him with all the details he needed to know — a penniless young girl with a worthless father would not survive long in this world without some visible means of support.

A girl like Lucy would not refuse his gold indefinitely. It was only a matter of time before the tedium of being his cousin's companion would overwhelm her, if it had not already, and then she would sing another tune, this time sweeter to his ears, to the accompaniment of the chink of his gold coins. What had his brother promised? A small establishment of her own, a maid and the means with which to maintain a modest lifestyle. Well, of one thing he was sure. He had the means, he had the money and, soon, he would have Lucy Walter as well.

In the safety of her bedroom that night, Lucy thought back over the events of the evening. She needed to be alone. The episode with Robert Sydney had been disquieting and wholly unexpected. How dare he regard her as a commodity to be bought and sold? It might only be his brother's money that separated her from penury, but that did not mean she would sell herself to the first bidder that came along.

Lucy was resting in her room, a few nights after the visit to Robert Sydney's house, idle thoughts occupying her mind, watching the flames from the fire illuminating the pretty Delft tiles, when a light tap was heard on her door. Thinking it was Anneka, calling her to say her mistress was ready to disrobe for the night, Lucy hurried to answer. But it was not Anneka who tapped, but Lord Herbert's valet.

'Lord Herbert wishes to see you in his study, Mistress Lucy.' Gathering her skirts around her and wrapping a shawl over her shoulders, Lucy stepped lightly down the backstairs and soon found herself facing her employer across his wide desk. He indicated to her to take a seat and she chose one close to the fire. Something in his manner made her uneasy and she could see indecision creased over his kindly face. He said nothing for a few moments, nervously fingering the diamond buttons on his embroidered waistcoat.

'Would you care for a glass of sack, my dear? I know the ladies are partial to sweet wine.'

He was making an attempt to speak lightly, but his hand was shaking as he gave her the glass.

'A small glass of wine for you and, I think, a large brandy for myself. You must be wondering why I asked to speak to you? I'll come straight to the point. I have a proposition to put to you.'

'A proposition?' said Lucy in bewilderment.

'Yes, I am acting on behalf of a kinsman of my wife's.'

Looking at the wide brown eyes of the girl in front of him, startled and afraid as a deer's, he felt sorry for her and wished, now, that he had not agreed to present her with this offer. Still, he had begun, and it was as well to get the business over with as quickly as possible.

'You made the acquaintance of Colonel Robert Sydney the other evening?'

Lucy nodded. It was all becoming clear now. It was Robert Sydney who was behind all this. If he had anything to say to her, why didn't he come himself and say it, instead of hiding behind Granville Herbert?

Lord Herbert was speaking again: 'Robert Sydney has taken an intense liking to you, Lucy, even, perhaps, fallen a little in love with you.'

He waited for Lucy to speak.

'You mean he wants to marry me?'

Lucy knew that was not Robert Sydney's meaning, but she wanted to see Lord Herbert's reaction to her words.

Evidently, the question had made him uncomfortable, and had made a difficult task even more burdensome.

Lucy realised the Herberts had been kind to her and what Granville Herbert was trying to say to her now was difficult for him.

'I think what you wish to convey to me, and are having difficulty in doing so, is that Robert Sydney wishes to buy me.'

Granville Herbert's face relaxed visibly. He was at once shocked and relieved by what Lucy had said. He felt very grateful to her for having said what he could not.

'You are not angry with me?' he asked.

Lucy shook her head. Her behaviour puzzled him, now he came to think about it.

Lucy seemed so innocent and when Robert Sydney had first approached him with the offer and told him what had transpired between Lucy and his brother, he had wondered if it was true, or if Sydney was lying to him. At first he had found the idea that Lucy could have accepted Algernon Sydney's money preposterous. Seeing her reaction now, he knew that Sydney had spoken the truth.

Sipping his brandy, to give himself a moment's respite, he wondered if Lord Glamorgan could have known how worldly Lucy was when he had recommended her as companion for Georgina. Was it the business to do with Sydney that had prompted him to say that taking Lucy under their wing would be an act of charity? He might never know. All he would vouch for was that not for a moment had Lucy brought them any vexation. Indeed, the girl had been a joy to have about the place.

'Now, if what I have divulged to you is distasteful, we can forget the whole matter.'

He paused, enquiringly, but Lucy said nothing.

'If, on the other hand, you wish to know more, then I can disclose the terms to you.'

Lucy learnt that what Robert Sydney was offering was, basically, what Algernon Sydney had offered.

'You need not decide immediately. Perhaps it would be best if you took a day or two to consider the whole matter and what is, essentially, a big step. Benefits to you would include having a benefactor and protector, which is not to say the same thing as a husband, but, still, no small matter for consideration. On the other hand, you can put Robert Sydney right out of your mind and his name need not be mentioned again in this house. You are welcome to make a home here, with Lady Herbert and myself. My wife is more than happy to have your company.'

His voice took on a conversational tone: 'We have no children of our own, as you know, and it has always been a great sadness to us. I think we feel it particularly now we are growing older.'

He kicked a dying log to life with his boot, sending a flurry of sparks eddying up the chimney.

'If you cared to stay with us, we would treat you as the daughter we would have liked to have had.'

His voice trailed away, old regrets filling his mind. Looking at him in the half light provided by the guttering candles, Lucy saw tiredness in his face and knew then that he was older than she had assumed him to be. She rose to her feet with an air of decisiveness.

'You have been very kind, Lord Herbert, and I appreciate what you have offered me in the way of a home. I have been very happy with you, but I hope you will understand my reasons for saying I need no time to consider Colonel Sydney's offer. Please tell him I accept.'

Relief swept over the old man's face. Whilst it was true he and his wife would have liked to keep Lucy with them, he feared she would soon tire of their narrow lives. A young woman like Lucy needed a life of her own.

'Robert Sydney is a generous man and, although a soldier by profession, I do not think that you will find him completely lacking in sensitivity. I would prefer to see you married but, in certain sections of society, marriage is a matter of fiscal and property transactions. It is a truism that money marries money. A girl without a dowry has no bargaining power, I'm afraid. My own dear wife was betrothed to me from an early age and I do not believe she loved me when we first married, but I like to think love has grown. You will not have a husband, but you will have a protector, which is the next best thing.'

* * *

And so it was that Lucy found herself the mistress of her own, quite delightful, town house. Decorated with wooden gables and an exuberance of sun-ripened honeysuckle, which clung to its walls, it resembled nothing so much as a doll's house. Although a modest dwelling compared to larger, more imposing residences in that leafy square, Lucy found it perfectly pleasing. Dappled sunlight filtered through the wooden shutters at the long windows, revealing a well-tended garden, where box and lavender had been clipped into neat hedges, vying with deep borders brimming with tulips, nasturtium, the beautiful, deep blue, love-in-a-mist tangling with the silvery seed pods of purple honesty, the whole punctuated by the graceful red maple and the glossy green leaves of the tulip tree.

Walking through the rooms, savouring the Persian and Turkish carpets on the floor, the silken shawls draped over small, side tables, the green, velvet-covered furniture, the stools, solid with nails, the oak table with ornamental legs, Lucy felt overwhelmed by the luxury of it all. She glanced at the glowing oil paintings on the walls, the work of the Flemish painters, and reflected that she might have acted a little hastily in accepting Sydney's offer, but opportunities like this did not present themselves very often. As Lord Herbert had said, a girl with neither money nor property had little choice. Besides, she could not contemplate a life spent with the Herberts, kind though they were.

To welcome Lucy to her new home, Robert Sydney had sent armfuls of tulips and they had been arranged in blue and white vases throughout the house. Upstairs, Lucy found fine

Egyptian cotton sheets on the beds and pillowcases frilled with Belgian lace and dripping with satin bows. The rooms were scented with the pungent smell of pomanders and Lucy saw, on opening the clothes closets and linen presses, that they were stuffed with Swiss lawn nightgowns, all exquisitely embroidered. On a bedside table lay a copy of the book entitled 'Paradisus'. It was with satisfaction that Lucy concluded Robert Sydney had not allowed his devotion to the Puritan cause, austere and frugal in many ways, to come between her and the finer things in life. She hoped she would not give him cause to regret the bargain.

Lucy's hands trembled as she opened the door to Robert Sydney, later that evening. Looking up into his face, she saw that the arrogant man she had met on that first occasion had been replaced by one who presented a completely different persona. Gone were the mocking eyes and the lips that touched hers lightly were undemanding and tender. 'I have brought you a present,' he said, reaching into his pocket.

'Open it,' he commanded, presenting her with a small box, daintly wrapped. Lucy felt a wave of pleasure sweep over her. All day she had been dreading this meeting and, at times, wondered if it had all been a terrible mistake, but now, all her forebodings had been swept aside within minutes of this man's arrival.

Sydney watched her closely as she undid the wrappings and ribbons. Carefully, she discarded the inner tissue paper then, gasping, pulled out an enamelled miniature brooch, with an indigo background and exquisite painted flowers in the centre. Encrusting the brooch were tiny diamonds which flashed blue, red, gold, green and yellow.

'Come here,' he said, pulling her gently towards him. 'Let me put it on for you.'

His right hand felt beneath the silky folds around her neckline and she was surprised at the pleasure she felt to feel his touch on her skin. He held the fichu away from her skin, fearing to prick her flesh. Her cheeks flushed, revealing her delight in this intimacy.

'Do you like it?'

She knew it must have cost a king's ransom and she loved it, not for its value, but for its own intrinsic beauty and because it was a gift he had chosen for her. Few gifts had come her way and this was a very special gift.

'I think it's lovely,' she replied. 'I was not expecting a present.'

'A lovely trinket, for my lovely girl,' he said softly, removing his cape and tossing it carelessly over the banister.

Watching him, Lucy marvelled that a man who had been rude and humiliating to her at their last meeting could be so thoughtful now. Indeed, tonight's events had changed her attitude towards Robert Sydney. She had viewed the package he had offered as a mere business agreement: she had something to offer him and she would let him have it, but at a price. Both sides understood this was a commercial venture, yet there might even be some form of emotional satisfaction in it, for both of them.

'I thought you might like to eat,' she said, indicating the dining-room. He nodded, putting his hand under her arm and guiding her into the opulent room. Candles glimmered in their sconces and highlighted the low bowls of hothouse flowers decorating the table. As she piled the food onto pewter platters and he poured the drinks, the thought crossed her mind that they presented as harmonious a picture of domesticity as was displayed in one of the Dutch interior paintings hanging on the wall. Looking up, he caught the smile on her face.

'Something is amusing you?'

It was not like Lucy to speak before thinking, but she was caught off her guard.

'I thought we looked for all the world like husband and wife.'

As soon as she said it, she regretted it. For a moment she thought she saw a frown darken his face, but she could not be sure, for when he looked up and spoke, no vestige of it remained and his tone was light.

'For all the world, we will be like husband and wife,' and he held her glance, till Lucy lowered her eyes in silent affirmation of his statement.

The deuce, but she looked so naive, so helpless, yet, in a harsh world, this girl had come this far by her own quick wits and her own sense of survival. Well, she was his now, to all intents and purposes, and he would see to it that she did not know want. All he asked was that she kept herself true to him and be available whenever he sought her company. In return she, and any issue, would have his protection.

They both ate hungrily, quickly devouring the cold chicken and tongue, which was followed by pastry letters filled with almond paste and sweetmeats. When she had finished her wine, Lucy put a golden apricot to her mouth and bit deeply into the centre, sinking her teeth into the pungent flesh, the juicy tang of the fruit filling the air. Taking a silver knife, Sydney cut himself a sliver of Gouda cheese, watching Lucy all the time. Her full red lips glistened with the overspill of juice and she put out a small pink tongue, which reminded him of a cat's, and slid it across her upper lip, savouring every droplet of sweetness, then closing her mouth and letting her tongue explore the fruit's smooth skin and luscious flesh. His mouth watered; she was utterly sensuous, her enjoyment of the fruit completely wanton. It boded well for their relationship, and he was pleased.

'Now, how do you like your new surroundings?' he asked briskly.

'Come, show me round. I will have the grand tour. I have seen it in the daytime many times, but I am sure it will look different at night, especially with you as my guide.'

He offered her his arm and they made their way through the little house, which was so perfect in every detail. Lucy found herself beginning to like Robert Sydney in a way she had not expected to.

Allowing himself to be led by Lucy, Sydney was gratified that Lucy was pleased with the way he had arranged things. Finally, she led him to her bedroom, dominated by the magnificent carved bed and matching cupboard made of time-blackened oak.

'If there is anything here not to your liking, I want you to tell me, Lucy.'

'I shall like it very much, I think' she replied.

Outside, the night had thrown a dark blanket over The Hague and Lucy pulled the heavy window hangings together, blotting out the blackness. The room was lit by the glow of the fire and one small, oil-burning lamp. Lucy turned, to see Sydney sitting on the bed, looking at her. Dropping to her knees, Lucy took his boots off, placing them neatly together. From the darkness, she heard his voice, low and commanding: 'Come, Lucy, kiss me and be mine,' he whispered. He cupped her breasts in his hands and felt the stiff nipples. He was glad she wanted him, too.

That night, Robert Sydney learnt that love is the sweetest passion, the cruellest mistress. Lucy took command of his heart, his soul, his body and Sydney, quite unexpectedly, fell in love. If she wanted him, he was entirely hers.

Lucy was generous with her body and gave him as much as he wanted, and more. Her heart, she kept for herself. There are two kinds of women: those who play for love, and those who play for money. Lucy now took the part of the latter.

As the skeins of a pale, golden dawn stretched out over The Hague, Robert Sydney took one last glance at Lucy, who was slumbering like a babe, before returning to his own dwelling. Sleep had bestowed an innocent, childlike quality to Lucy's face, which was at variance with what he knew about Lucy. She had so nearly been Algernon's, but that thought would not trouble him now that she was his. He concluded his brother's loss had been his gain and as for his bargain with Lucy, he was well satisfied.

Lucy breakfasted late that morning. She sipped her bowl of chocolate, dipping her roll into it and stretching out her shapely legs in a long, luxuriant gesture. The previous night she had seen a side of Sydney's character that had been unexpected. She had not expected him to treat her as other than a servant, but he had made an attempt at wooing her. The enamelled brooch had delighted her and it was as fine a gift as any lord might present to his lady. She was beginning to like Sydney more than she would ever have thought possible at this time yesterday.

Lucy had just come out of her bath at noon, when there was a loud rapping at the door. The maid hastened to answer it. A short while later she appeared in Lucy's boudoir with an armful of red roses, which bore a note with Sydney's signature.

Lucy was feeling more contented than she had for a long time. Holland was a place she could become fond of. London had disappointed her, but in Holland, people lived more freely, the burgher class was becoming prosperous and commissioning artists like Van Dyck and Reubens to paint for them. In this atmosphere of expansion and prosperity Lucy felt alive and invigorated. Life, and all it had to offer, lay before her.

Chapter 5

It was July, 1648. An air of serenity hung over The Hague and found its echo in Lucy's heart. Her face wore that expression so commonly found on the visages of those who have little more taxing in life than merely to be, to exist, to please and be pleased. Mistress of her own household, she was content and, if she had stopped to think about her position that bright, summer's day, could think of nothing more pleasant than to be who she was.

With Robert Sydney as her considerate lover, she was given the kind of attention she craved.

'I have money to spend, servants to command. Civil war may be raging in England, but, quite frankly, it does not concern me one iota,' she remarked one day to Georgina Herbert, over the teacups.

The older woman smiled indulgently; she was glad to see Lucy blooming. 'I think, if the world were yours to command, you would be content to stay in Holland forever, Lucy.'

The following week, when she was dressing, Lucy made her mind up. She could feel her gown of linen flax pulling tightly against her breasts, which were tender and full. Tonight she would tell him. It might come as a surprise to him or perhaps he had already guessed. But then again, men were often stupid in such matters. She clasped her hands over her round little belly, to protect the new life it held, to keep it secret and safe from the world a little while again.

'Women know when they are pregnant before the doctor does,' she remembered her mother saying. Lucy's pregnancy had come as no surprise to her. Her body was behaving in a way that was unfamiliar to her, yet did not surprise her.

'I ate more than a man and slept day and night, too, if I had the chance, when I was expecting you,' her mother had told her.

A few weeks ago Lucy was agile and strong, but now she was careful not to lift weights. How quickly one modifies one's behaviour when the need arises, she reflected.

It was late that evening, when Sydney was reclining in his night shirt on the lavishly trimmed lace pillows and Lucy sat brushing her hair with the silver chased hair brush, that his eyes lingered on her. He was, indeed fortunate in having Lucy. Even viewing Lucy against a background of costly furnishings and arrayed as she was in her delicate night attire, she retained a vulnerable, waif-like quality. It was this mix of innocence and carnal knowledge, not found in many of her class, that appealed so strongly to him. There were things about her that he would, perhaps, never understand. Her willingness to sell herself, first to his brother, then to him: two men she had not known. Granted, other women had done much the same thing, but it was still difficult for a man to understand. An arranged marriage was a different matter, for it was the parents who chose the best match they could find. Lucy was still but a child, and it appeared she had no one in the world to appeal to for guidance. Just as well she was his, for he would protect her. And that was another thing he liked about her, the feelings of tenderness she aroused in him. He could get a woman, of a sort, off the streets any day and in his time he had. Money was all they asked for the satisfaction they gave. He sighed. He was glad he had passed the stage when, as a youth, it had been an adventure, a test of manhood and daring, to approach a whore. He had tired of that game, and before he had caught anything, luckily. Maturity had brought a need for more than temporary gratification. It was loneliness, a sense of isolation, that had led him to the need for Lucy. The thought of her filled his days with purpose and he had come to think of her as his wife in The Hague. If she were to be with child, then that would please him, too. They had been together eight weeks now and he expected, sooner or later, to make her fat.

Outside, the organ grinder trundled by and the busiest birds prepared to relinquish their day's labours. Lucy's face, silhouetted against the windows, assumed a solemn expression.

'I have something to tell you, Robert.'

His heart leapt, but he would not betray his hopes yet. Instead, he heard his voice asking, teasingly:

'What do you have to tell me, sweetling? Is it that you do not like this house, you no longer love me and you wish with all your heart you were back in London?'

She pouted momentarily, not realising that it was his joke. Then her face cleared and she understood. She walked over to him, laid her head upon his chest and encircled his neck with her arms.

'No, of course not. You know I think this is the prettiest house imaginable, I love you to distraction and I do not miss England.'

The first and last statements were true, the honesty of the middle one dubious, for Lucy was one of those women who could receive love, return it in a limited way and at the same time keep her heart for herself.

'Well, what is it that is so important that you have to tell me?'

Again she hesitated.

'Whisper it in my ear, Lucy, that we two alone will share your secret.'

And so, with her soft lips against his ear, Robert Sydney learnt that Lucy would bear their child, to be born in the late spring of the following year. Then he planted softest kisses on her face and neck and nursed her in his arms, as though she were his baby. Night's soft folds descended and swaddled the lovers as they lay in each others' arms. Sydney was gentle and tender with Lucy, for he wanted no harm to come to the child that was his, growing within her.

* * *

Lucy had not heard for a while from the Herberts, for Lady Herbert had not been well of late. She was at that certain time in life which can be hard for a woman. Bright and sparkly one day, the next all would be doom and gloom and Granville Herbert had become perplexed by Georgina's behaviour.

'If only she could keep a steady course,' he had been heard to lament.

It was on another of those sunshine yellow days that Lucy had grown to love, when Anneka, the maid, arrived with a note from Granville Herbert, asking Lucy to pay them a visit, which was sure to cheer Georgina up. Reading it, Lucy remembered the Herberts' unfailing kindness to her. She could not refuse someone on whom she had come to look as a friend. The invitation had invited her to take tea at three in the afternoon the next day.

The following morning Lucy chose a basket of fruit from the conservatory, which she hoped would tempt her friend's appetite, then asked the cook to make a deep Dutch apple tart, spiced with cinnamon, sweetened with brown sugar and glazed with butter, for her to take with her. She chose a gown of dark navy stuff, which would not attract attention to her shape. Already she was conscious of filling out and if her burgeoning body did not give her away, then her glowing good health would.

Arriving at the Herberts' home, which was so familiar to her, Lucy was relieved to find Georgina having a good day. Kissing Lucy on the cheek, she led her into her own, small sitting room.

'If I were not feeling better, the sight of you would certainly have cheered me up, my dear. Now, how is my cousin Sydney treating you? No, don't answer that, for I can see he is treating you very well.'

'I am enjoying my new way of life, but I often think of you,' replied Lucy. 'I am far happier now than I ever was in England.'

Lady Herbert poured them some China tea and cut thick slices of plum cake to go with it. Sipping her tea, she said: 'My husband has an unexpected visitor. A very important guest,' and she arched her eyebrows to add emphasis to what she had just said. A short pause, and then, watching Lucy's face closely, she said: 'Charles Stuart.'

Georgina Hebert thoroughly enjoyed the startled look that broke over Lucy's face.

'Not expecting that, were you? I knew that would surprise you, and it did, didn't it? Granville has been active in gaining support for the King's cause, mainly financial, of course. The poor King is at present a prisoner at Carisbrooke Castle,' she explained.

'How fares the prince since last I met him here?' enquired Lucy.

'Well enough in himself, I believe, but I have not spoken with him this day. He is with Granville in his study.'

With that, the door burst open and Granville Herbert stood before them, with the Prince at his side. Rising hastily, Georgina Herbert dropped a deep curtsey, Lucy quickly following her lead. Granville Herbert spoke: 'The prince has honoured us with a visit and I told him he must join the ladies for tea, if only very briefly.'

'Indeed you must, Sire,' said Georgina, ringing the bell for the maid. Lucy sat in her chair, wishing to be inconspicuous, yet longing for the Prince to notice her. She had no need to worry, though, for the Prince had noticed her and Lucy, in her pregnancy, looked more beautiful than ever.

'May I present Mistress Lucy Walter,' said Georgina, when she noticed the Prince's eyes fixed on Lucy.

'Ah, I believe we met when I last was here,' said the Prince.

'I was here but I did not think that you would remember me, Sire,' said Lucy.

Georgina was busying herself with the tea and her husband was drawing up extra chairs. Glancing at their hosts, and aware that they were preoccupied, the Prince took Lucy's hand and lightly brushed it with his lips. In a low voice, meant only for her ears, he replied so quietly only she could hear: 'How could I forget you?'

Lucy felt her heart pounding and in that moment, neither had eyes deep enough to contain all the emotions their souls felt. There is always one moment in any relationship, when a man and a woman acknowledge they have found their other self. For Lucy and Charles Stuart it happened in the sun-filled sitting room of the comfortably married Herberts. Call it fate, destiny, the work of the gods or what you will, but both knew they had recognised the devastating attraction each held for the other. It was a moment frozen in time, but only a moment, for Granville Herbert's words, offering Charles a chair, forced their thoughts back to the present. Polite, light-hearted conversation ensued, in which Lucy took little part. She sat quietly, in the knowledge that she and the Prince shared something that the other couple in the room were completely unaware of.

Lucy returned home shortly afterwards, telling Sydney nothing of her visit to the Herberts and her encounter with Charles Stuart. This omission on Lucy's part was in keeping with her character. There was that serenity about her that did not give way to idle talk. Equally, she knew when it was wisest to keep silent and deemed the Prince's visit best not mentioned.

Sydney was pleased that Lucy's pregnancy had not diminished her need for him and he settled into a relationship which he believed had something of permanence about it. One night, having exhausted himself with passion for Lucy, he lay loosely entwined with her. Tired as he was, sleep eluded him. England was in the grip of the second outbreak of civil war. News had come from Algernon that six men o'war had revolted at Deal in favour of the King and were anchored off the Dutch coast.

They had been joined by thirteen other vessels and Charles Stuart had hurried to Helvoetsluys to take command. They were now sailing for England and Sydney could only imagine that the Prince's first action would be to rescue his father from Carisbrooke Castle. If the king were to be freed, who knew what the outcome of the war might be? A captured king made a poignant figure, but boded well for the Parliamentarian cause. A free king would rally support for his own cause and weaken the strength of the Parliamentarians. He rolled over and looked at Lucy, slumbering as though she had not a care in the world. That was how he wanted things to stay for her. A woman's job was to please a man and bring up their children. War should be outside a woman's experience. He kissed her sleeping eyelids. He was not sorry Algernon was busying himself in the Parliamentarian effort for, as far as Lucy was concerned, his brother's loss had been his delight. He wondered about Lucy's feelings. Would she have loved his brother just as passionately? He would probably never know and was glad he would not.

During the next few days Lucy felt unsettled. She attributed it to her chance meeting with the Prince. She had been satisfied living with Sydney, in a humdrum way. She knew she would never love him in the way she had dreamt she would love a man when she lay under the trees in the hot summers of long ago in Roch. Then she believed she would fall passionately in love and give her heart and soul to one man for ever and ever, but Richard Palmer had soon faded from her memory. For Lucy, this was the time when she came to realise idealism was all very well when one could afford it but what was practical was more important if one had no money. In Pembrokeshire, the only chance of a good marriage for her was with her Barlow cousins, and she did not want anyone, not even relatives, to marry her out of charity alone. Seeing Charles Stuart the other afternoon had released feelings that made her feel uncomfortable.

With Sydney, her feelings were a thing apart. She was grateful to him for what he provided and repaid him in kind. She acted lovingly and disguised the fact that she did not feel loving. With the Prince, she could not begin to count the number of ways in which she had been aware of him. His dark, vagabond looks had remained a constant memory, from that first time she had seen him in Golden Grove, and she had never forgotten them, even when his features had become a blur in her mind. Had it been the shape of his mouth, the squareness of his shoulders or the incomprehensibility of his eyes that lingered and pleased her most? When he had bent to kiss her hand, she had smelt the sweetness of his breath and it had wafted a strange excitement. All she could do was to try and forget him, for he could only be a dream to her. She must try to concentrate on what she had with Robert Sydney. Her only complaint was that she did not love him. One could not have everything, and she accepted that she was luckier than most. The child would create a stronger bond between them, especially if it were to be a boy.

'Lucy,' said Sydney one day, a frown clouding his face, 'I have business in England and must be gone a short while.'

Seeing her startled expression, he kissed her on the forehead.

'I will not be gone long. You can continue as you are now, until I return. Have plenty of rest, for I will not be here to disturb your nights.' He laughed and put his arms around her. She wondered what it was that made him leave her so suddenly, but thought it best not to ask.

'I leave on the evening tide and I shall bring my Lucy gifts when I return and baby clothes fit for any king's child. Take care of yourself and the child,' he said, patting her stomach. 'I'll not forget pretty things for the babe.'

His arms tightened around her. It grieved him sorely to

leave her, for she had come to fill a part of every thought he had, but there was need to return for supplies of money. Keeping Lucy in this state was a costly business. A lingering kiss and he was gone.

At first, Lucy missed her lover. She had not made friends within the small English community that existed in The Hague, believing it best that a woman in her position keep in the background. That way, less questions were asked and life was easier. Her only real friends in The Hague were the Herberts. Between herself and the servants, she kept a distance, believing it unwise to become too familiar. The thought of what had happened betweeen her father and one of the serving maids haunted her.

July gave way to hot, flower frilled August. When Lucy had the energy, she began some fine sewing for the baby's layette. She blest Marie now for forcing her to learn to sew. Her words came back to her: 'All the finest ladies in the land can sew.'

Well, if the baby had to rely on its mother to sew its entire layette, it would scarcely have a thing to wear, she thought ruefully, for she was a slow worker. Just as well Sydney had promised to return with clothes fit for a prince.

She wrapped her sewing in a pillowcase and put it away. She must be careful to keep it from her servants' prying eyes. Only that morning she had been aware of the cook's eyes on her body.

Opening the clothes closet, Lucy inspected her dresses. Before long she would have to let out the seams. By December she would be halfway through her pregnancy and a large shawl would serve to conceal her state, if she were lucky. She yawned. A stretch on the bed would be pleasant for an hour or so. It was as she removed her slippers that she became aware of a man's voice in the hall. Robert could not be back so soon, surely, he had scarcely been gone for more than two weeks, and he had said not to expect him back for a month or more. But it was not Robert's voice she heard, for this voice was of a lighter timbre.

Quickly, she tidied her appearance, smoothing her skirts around her and rubbing her cheeks to make them glow. Soon, Gerda knocked on the door.

'Madame, an English gentleman to see you. I have shown him into the front sitting room.'

Lucy felt her heart pounding. If an accident had befallen Sydney, where did that leave her and the child? Despite knowing she was not to rush, she ran down the stairs and flung open the sitting room doors. Seeing who her visitor was, she came to an abrupt halt and a look of astonishment broke out over her face, for none other than Charles Stuart stood there. Remembering her manners just in time, she gave a low curtsey.

'Your Highness, I am honoured,' she murmured.

'Let me help you,' said Charles, taking her arm and steadying her until she was standing upright again.

'Forgive me for calling on you in this way, but the truth is, Mistress Lucy, after our last meeting, I have scarce stopped thinking of you,' and he looked at her with a twinkle in his eye.

Lucy's head was reeling. She could not believe what she was hearing. Seeing her blushes and confusion, the Prince was equal to the moment, 'Ah, I know that is the type of thing you hear every day a hundred times and more, I have no doubt; and if you were to say so, then I should not be in the least surprised.'

Lucy attempted to behave as calmly as was possible under the circumstances. She felt rooted to the spot. The sight of him, the sound of his voice, his presence, was all more than she could comprehend. Then she heard herself say: 'Pray take a seat, sire. Would you have some sucket, or a posset? I can send for the maid.'

'No, I thank you kindly, but my business here must needs be short. Colonel Sydney does not support my cause and for that reason I would not linger unduly. I have intelligence that he is away at the moment and so I have called, for my business is not with him, but with you, Lucy.'

He used her name as though they were old acquaintances, with a shared past history.

He lowered his voice and it took on an urgency.

'I did not joke when I said you filled my thoughts. From that first time I saw you in Golden Grove, I never completely forgot you. Always you remained, lingering in my mind, like a dream that I wanted to recall, but could not.' He paused and looked at her. 'Do you understand what I am saying or am I a fool who should be quietened at all costs?'

Later, Lucy was to recall she could not remember what she had said by way of reply, but she, too, had experienced the magic that appeared when the two of them were in each others' presence. So, this force which was real for her, had touched him, too.

Pulling his chair closer to hers, he caught both her hands.

'Lucy, the life I lead is dangerous. Years of my youth have been spent avoiding danger. Each day that comes, for all I know, could be my last, but I pray God it will not be. I am lately returned from England. In vain I tried to rescue my father and my hope is that still I may. Many things went against me — the defeat of Royalist troops at Preston this very month, the indiscipline of the sailors who turned sides . . .'

He drew his hand over his face and Lucy thought that one so young should not have had to bear so many burdens, but thought it best to say nothing. Charles, too, was silent for a moment, contemplating the play of sunlight on the carpet, as though his despair knew no depths.

Catching Lucy's glance, his face brightened.

'Lucy, what I am asking, is that you leave your Puritan Colonel and come to me, be my wife in all but name.'

What Charles Stuart had just said was unbelievable. 'Be a wife to me in all but name.' Was he mad, insane, had the strain of recent events turned his mind? Lucy looked at him carefully. He seemed sane enough. What if she were to reply in the affirmative and then he were to withdraw his offer in a day or two? Well, no damage would have been done and she could continue her life with Sydney as though nothing had happened and he would be none the wiser. She got up and went to the window, the Prince's eyes following her all the time. What she had with Sydney was too good to lose, yet there was no depth to the relationship, for she could never love him. All she felt was gratitude and whilst gratitude might not be such a bad emotion on which to found a relationship, yet it could never be a substitute for love. That feeling that out of all the time in the world, from its beginning to its end, two souls had come together at one unique moment and had fired each other's senses, caused their hearts to leap together, recognising each other out of all the other people that existed. What was love? Perhaps she would never be able to answer with certainty, but she knew what it was not. The nights when she had lain with Sydney, wondering how her body could be so numb, so dead, when his was throbbing with desire. The times when he had wanted to love her all night and her only wish was that he would be quickly satisfied. He filled her arms at night, but in the day, she never longed for the night, yearned for his body or desired his presence.

Charles Stuart was standing behind her now and his arms encircled her waist. That was another thing that could not be overlooked for long: Robert Sydney's baby. Should she tell the Prince, or not? There was always the possibility that she might miscarry, many women did. If she mentioned the baby and then miscarried, she would have been a fool to herself.

If we are lucky, moments of clarity come to us and we see the future, if only partially, at key points in our lives. Lucy experienced such a moment that afternoon, in that sun-dappled room. Turning, she lifted her lips to those of the Prince and in so doing acknowledged to herself that she had found the true love of her life. How does such recognition occur? It is not given to many to know, but both realised that they had found their other, true self.

'Lucy, I will send for you tonight. Can you be ready?' he asked anxiously.

'I will be ready,' she replied gravely.

When Charles had departed, her heart was in turmoil. The future King of England had visited her and had asked her to live with him as his wife in all but name. Yet, she was sure that her decision had been the correct one to take. As far as Sydney was concerned, she felt she owed him nothing. Quickly, she began to pack her more valuable possessions, including the enamelled brooch Sydney had given her on that first night together. She felt no regrets that she might never see him again; in fact, she hoped she would never see him again.

Money had bought her and money could buy him another woman. She must follow the dictates of her heart. Charles Stuart offered her a love she was able to return and this she could not dismiss. As for the baby, she was only a few weeks advanced and the child might be Charles's, for all anyone would know. At the moment, the baby was a mere detail and it could not be allowed to stand in the way of their love. She would have liked her first child to have been the Prince's, but circumstances had conspired against her and there was nothing she could do about it now.

'Gerda, Gerda,' Lucy called to the maid. 'I am going away for a few days and need you to pack a few of my things.'

The maid wondered whether her mistress's hasty departure had anything to do with the visit of the English gentleman, but said nothing.

It took less than an hour for Lucy to remove all trace of herself from that bijou of a house that had so delighted her a mere handful of weeks ago. Outside, a carriage awaited her, with the cypher of Prince William of Orange, Charles's brother-in-law, on the door. The coachman took her luggage and Lucy settled back in the seat, pulling together the heavy curtains and was gone, not sparing a glance for the house that had given her a period of tranquillity in a life that was to prove turbulent.

The moon sailed in and out of the clouds as the carriage bowled along. Approaching a wooded area, where long shadows stretched across the road like ghostly fingers on the walls of a deserted house, Lucy was glad there were not many miles left to go, for it had been a lonely journey, with little traffic in either direction. Was it the nervousness of a pregnant woman, or was it intuition, for she felt apprehensive about something. The horse was neighing, shaking its head and jangling the harness as though it sensed danger and Lucy could hear the driver speaking soothingly to it.

Suddenly, out of the darkness, sprang a highwayman, not a gentleman robber, but a ruffian on horseback.

'Stop!' came the command, sharp as a stab of pain.

Lucy felt her heart thumping against her ribs.

'You wait where you are,' he called to the driver. The single occupant of the carriage was a woman, and a pretty one at that. There was more than money to be had out of this night's plundering. The highwayman edged his horse alongside the carriage and ordered Lucy to get out.

Her stomach lurched at his next words.

'On your way,' he said tersely to the driver.

'Lady, you come with me.'

Swift as a shot from a pistol, a voice rang out, 'The lady waits where she is.'

Turning his head, the robber saw a dark, swarthy man, with the looks of a gypsy king, but with a dangerous air of authority about him.

'Move, before your horse feels my sword.'

The man needed no further bidding. Digging his heels into his steed's ribs, he wheeled and turned the horse, then swiftly spurred him away.

'We will not require your services any further tonight, Sir,' said Charles to the coach driver, who had waited a little further on.

'I shall see the lady safely home.'

Despite the recent terrors, Lucy displayed no signs of distress.

'I must thank Your Highness for coming to my aid.'

'Madam, it was only what any gentleman would have done,' and Charles bowed, adopting the attitude of a gallant. Changing his tone and becoming serious, he said, 'Come Lucy, we must away from here. We have both had enough adventure for one night.'

* * *

'Shall I pour?' Lucy glanced at Charles. His face was in shadow and his expression inscrutable. When he spoke, his words thrilled her.

'I have no need of wine with you, Lucy,' and emotion thickened his voice.

One step and he was across the room, his strong arms carrying her to the bed and laying her down. They came together, neither of them innocents to the act of love, yet it was as though they had not loved anyone else before. Their bodies burst into fire and Lucy marvelled that such rapture could exist. Again and again, Charles exhausted himself. No woman could have wished for a more ardent lover. When Charles had spent all his strength, he was still able to love her one last time.

When Charles awoke, he remembered the bliss of the night.

'As far as I am concerned, you are my wife,' he whispered in Lucy's ear, mingling his words with kisses. It was neither here nor there to him that they were not married in the eyes of the Church. A loving God would not condemn a man for a little irregular pleasure. His mother's maids-of-honour had laughed openly when the Chaplain-in-Waiting had read the Epistle of that miserable misogynist Saint Paul, regarding the relationship between love and constancy.

Lucy said nothing, but scooped a silver spoonful of caviar into Charles's mouth. It was best to enjoy what was freely given, without questioning or asking for more. To love and be loved was a joy, not a sin. Only the other week, Blaise Pascal, the philosopher, had said the greatest of evils was civil war. She did not ask that Charles marry her and make her his Queen. They were living in parlous times. Charles might not even live to inherit the throne of England, always assuming there would be a throne to inherit, the way things were going.

Charles did not trouble himself with what Sydney might think or do when he found that Lucy had left him.

'All's fair in love and war' was as good a motto as any and he knew a little about the two states. As long as Lucy was happy with him, he would be well content. He would be as true to her as he could be, but he was unable to promise eternal fidelity, for he had that type of nature that could love more than one woman at a time. He saw nothing wrong in sharing his love around; love did not have to be exclusively for one person, to make it valid. A father was able to love more than one child and a man could love more than one woman at a time; it was as simple as that. The Church might ask for fidelity, but he would live by his own rules.

Summer gave way to gaudy autumn. Robert Sydney returned from England, his appetite for Lucy increased by his absence. An ominous silence hung over the home they had shared, when he entered.

'Lucy, Lucy,' he called, urgently, but no Lucy came running. His heart was heavy as stone, fearing some catastrophe had occurred in his absence, even that Lucy was dead. The maid avoided his eyes.

'Gerda, where is your mistress? Where is Mistress Lucy? Do you know, woman?'

The maid held out her hands and shrugged her shoulders in a hopeless gesture.

'If you know, tell me.' His voice rose. 'Has harm come to her?'

They were joined by the cook, startled by the noise. She had never been fond of Lucy.

'It is said she lives with the English Prince Charles, whose sister is married to our Prince William of Orange, Sir.'

All his worst fears came together. Lucy had gone. Lucy, his own, darling Lucy, preferred being a Prince's harlot to a Colonel's kept woman. He had not expected to love Lucy, but he did. Whatever she had felt for him was, quite clearly, something else.

'Are the reports true?' He hated having to ask the servants, but had little choice.

'All The Hague is talking of it, if not all Holland.'

It was more than he could bear. The blood seethed through his veins, tensing the muscles in his neck, causing his head to throb. He saw the women looking at him with interest. Pride came to his aid. He would not show the servants he cared and when the cook began talking again, he cut her short.

'That will be all. You may return to your work, the two of you.'

In his study, Sydney poured a glass of whisky. Sickened as he was, he would not grieve for long. Better to show her faithlessness now, than after the child was born. Obviously, loyalty had been too much to expect of Lucy. Writing to Algernon, he concealed his grief, merely telling him, briefly, that Lucy had gone. In a display of bravado, he concluded.

'Let who will have her, for she is already sped.'

He sealed the letter, but the words 'For she is already sped,' kept repeating themselves in his mind. He had wanted the child so much, but he was determined to banish Lucy and her precious cargo from his mind. Henceforward, Charles Stuart could look after Lucy. Would she be faithful to her royal lover, he wondered. Only time would tell.

* * *

'Are you happy with me, Lucy?'

The sun was making valiant efforts to push open the

curtains as Charles lay in bed, his arms entwined around Lucy, his lips nuzzling her breasts.

'Lucy, answer me.'

For answer, she closed his lips with kisses.

'I could wish to be kept in better style,' she teased, but seeing the furrow that puckered his brow, she hastened to reassure him.

'I am very happy with you,' and she spoke the truth, for she dearly loved her 'Black Boy', which was her pet name for Charles. He fulfilled her as no other man had.

'Do I make you happy?'

His arms tightened around her.

'These are worrying times for me, but just being with you and holding you eases my troubles.'

He fell silent for a moment before saying: 'How would you like to visit Paris? I would like to see my mother and little sister, Minette. We could go before winter makes travelling difficult.'

The idea appealed greatly to Lucy. She was always ready for new adventures.

It was a fine autumn day, sunny but lacking summer's warmth, when they arrived in Paris. Despite being warned that street fighting was likely to break out at any time, for there was much trouble with the Fronde and Charles's young cousin, Louis XIV and all the Royal family of France, had been obliged to take refuge in Saint Germain, Lucy was enraptured with Paris. As they approached Henrietta Maria's apartments, Lucy gasped: 'Oh, Charles, I never dreamt the Louvre was so beautiful, or that just one city in the world could be so lovely.'

Charles smiled indulgently at her.

'Lucy, you delight in everything. I think I see things anew when I am with you.'

And it was true, for she viewed things in a fresh way and he felt renewed by her enthusiasm.

Henrietta Maria was visibly moved to see her first born child again.

Charles had always been her most dearly loved child and seeing him now, after an absence of months, reminded her painfully of her husband, a prisoner in Carisbrooke Castle.

'Charles, you remind me so much of your father, when he was a young man and I a young bride.'

Her words pleased Charles. He cared not whether he resembled his father in looks, but he did care that he made his mother happy and for a few moments, at least, Henrietta Maria was happy.

Lucy stood apart from the little group who stood embracing each other, the queen looking so frail and old, it seemed impossible that she had given birth to a child as young as her daughter Minette now was.

Henrietta Maria was everything Lucy imagined a queen should be, warm, yet a little distant, dignified, yet never able to forget, even with the son she loved so dearly, that she was the wife of a king. Though she was reduced to poverty, she was used to obeisance, to being treated differently from other women.

'Ah! Charles,' she said, pulling him to her, running her thin fingers through the curling locks in the way she had when he was a baby, and they occupied another world, and she and his father had idolised the dark-skinned baby, born to be heir to the throne of England. She kissed his cheeks and looked searchingly at him. He was a man now, but as far as she was concerned, he would never cease to be her baby boy.

She drew Charles to a chair by the fire. It was not every day that she and Minette could light a good fire. For them, the necessities of life had become a luxury. If they had not been pitied by the English abbot, Walter Montagu, their plight would have been even more dire; as it was, she could not bear Charles having to see them in their present poverty.

'To think that I, daughter of the great Henri Quatre, should be treated like this, in my own country, is disgraceful. Mon Dieu! The blood of the Bourbons runs in our veins,

Charles, never forget that. Your father is a King, your grandfather, Henri of Navarre, was a King of France and you, you will be a King one day.'

Her voice trailed away, as though she had no emotion left. Charles looked at her pityingly. He had heard it whispered that it was Henrietta Maria who was responsible for the plight in which his father now found himself. If she had not encouraged him to defy Parliament in the way he had, then they might all now be in England, in St. James's Palace, leading the lives of a King's family, and not unwanted refugees on the Continent. But he still felt sorry that one person should have suffered as much as his mother had. Her pride and stubbornness was not a trait her eldest son had inherited, however, and it was one of Charles's saving graces that he would tack and veer with the wind, change course if it was necessary to maintain peace in England and a Stuart on the throne.

'And how is my little sister, Minette, who is not as little now as I remembered her to be,' said Charles. He held out his arms and Minette leapt into them. It was good to hold a child, to feel the youthful glee that was in her.

'Charles, who is that?' said his sister pointing at Lucy.

This last question drew a sharp remark from Henrietta Maria, who despite all her worries was determined that Minette should learn the manners of a princess.

'Has Morton omitted to tell you that it is rude to point, madam?'

Putting Minette down carefully on her feet, Charles drew Lucy forward.

'Mama, this is Mistress Lucy Walter. Her father's castle in Wales was used to billet the Cavaliers.'

On hearing this last sentence, his mother's face softened. She had no use for anyone who was not actively involved in the King's struggle, but here was a girl whose family was helping in the fight against Cromwell. The queen stretched out her hand.

'I am glad to welcome you, Mistress Walter. I would we had met in happier circumstances.'

Henrietta Maria chose not to enquire too closely into the relationship between Charles and Lucy, but she could guess they were lovers. Henrietta Maria's husband had always been faithful to her, not so much out of a moral choice but because it was not a part of his nature to seek his pleasures in another woman's bed. Her son Charles, she suspected, was very like her father, Henri, very taken with the smile of a pretty woman, the beckoning warmth in her eyes, the splay of her hips. Well, Charles had come to bring her comfort, not to receive her judgement, and she would not spoil the occasion by censuring the one whom she loved so much.

'Mama has had to suffer too much,' said James, Charles's younger brother, who had recently escaped and joined Henrietta Maria and Minette in the Louvre. 'I fear she makes very poor company for Minette. When I came here, she was overcome with grief that Elizabeth and Henry were unable to escape with me. I had to explain to her that Elizabeth was weakened after the accident to her leg and Henry was too young to undergo the hazards involved, but it fair broke my heart to have to do so.'

'I see no reason why we should not all spend the winter in The Hague with William and Mary,' said Charles. 'Our sister Mary would like us to stay with her. Aunt Elizabeth of Bohemia is already there and Mama would be much happier away from this cold, draughty place,' he said, indicating the large, barn-like room. 'Indeed, I am grateful to William for being so generous with his hospitality. I often avail myself of it — that is, when I do not make myself comfortable elsewhere,' he said, indicating Lucy, his eyes twinkling.

James, young as he was, understood his brother's meaning. When he was more settled, he would find himself a woman, too.

'Mama, forget for a moment that you are the daughter of a King of France.'

It was Charles speaking, and exasperation was in his voice.

'Think of yourself, and if you have no care for yourself, think of Minette.'

'Charles, I have made up my mind. I will have no more of your suggestions. Minette and I are waiting in Paris. That is all I will say.'

Charles sighed. His mother was so stubborn. He knew when he was beaten.

The winter of 1648 was very cold, but Lucy was comfortable in the small house Charles had provided for her. She did not go out during the day as frequently as she had in the summer, for she was content to spend the days of the middle part of her pregnancy quietly. Charles visited her often. Whether or not he truly believed the child was his, she did not know, but he took a pride in her pregnancy, and visited her regularly. Towards the middle of December he arrived with a grave look on his face. Lucy knew the news from England must be very bad for Charles to look so downcast.

'The Rump,' he said, referring to the Parliament, 'has voted the King be tried for high treason.' He let out a ragged breath. 'I never believed they would do it, not in England, not to their King.'

He paused for a moment, a faraway look in his eyes. His voice was wistful when he spoke, 'If only I could have rescued him from Carisbrooke, if only everything had not conspired against me.'

'Stop torturing yourself in this way. You did what you could to rescue him, no-one could have done more.' Lucy's voice softened. 'Come to me,' said Lucy, putting her arms around her 'Black Boy'.

'My father is a good man, Lucy, a good king and a good father.'

Lucy could only nod in agreement. She had no interest in the affairs of state and cared little and knew even less about the King's quarrel with Parliament, his imposition of unjust taxes, his sympathy for the Roman Catholic Church and his unswerving belief in the divine right of kings. All Lucy knew was that she hated to see Charles unhappy.

Taking him by the hand, she led him upstairs and comforted him in the way she new best.

Charles was desperately short of money, but he always found funds to keep Lucy in a modest form of comfort. Not only that, he had her portrait painted over and over. His favourite was of a voluptuous Lucy, scantily clad, one naked breast bared, the rest of her lovely body loosely swathed in silken folds of material and cupid peeping out from behind a curtain.

'It is your likeness only I wish to see in a painting, your face when I close my eyes, only your eyes and mouth I want in my dreams and all my waking moments, too,' he said taking her in his arms.

'I wonder that you would even cast a glance in my direction. Even my mother called me her ugly baby, much as she loved me. Is it because I am a prince that you take me as your lover?' he asked anxiously.

Lucy shook her head. She had many faults, but she was truthful.

'I love you Charles. Titles do not concern me. You are my Black Boy and will never be ugly to me.'

Lucy was happy with Charles in a way she never had been with Sydney. There were women who craved titles, but Lucy was not one of those. When she loved, she gave her heart and she had given hers to Charles. Anyway, it was not hard to love Charles. Almost any woman could, he was so gentle and loving. He made it clear to Lucy in a hundred ways that he loved her, and he also told her, over and over. When Charles was born, Venus the planet of love, had been in the ascendant, so how could Charles fail to be anything but the ideal lover. Charles I had been handsome in a delicate sort of way, but his son, swarthy and dark as a gypsy's child, was to the taste of most women, with hard good looks that came from having been a fugitive, and forced to live by his wits, for many years.

Christmas time was fast approaching, but Charles was too miserable to care. The festive season was at odds with his feelings.

'I would give anything, do anything, if it would ensure the release of my father,' he told Lucy.

Messengers were sent to England, bearing a blank sheet of paper, signed only 'Charles P'. Many times successive blank sheets were sent, but when Charles received no answer, he realised that was his reply. There would be no negotiations over the fate of Charles I.

Charles was joined by Lucy, in William and Mary's palace in The Hague, for what could only be a solemn Christmas-tide. Brother and sister found comfort in each other's company and clung to the faint belief that the English people would never kill their king.

'Sovereignty must surely prevail over the will of Parliament,' avowed Mary. With all his heart, Charles wished that he could agree with her, but many doubts troubled his nights and denied him sleep. What little hope he harboured was finally destroyed when intelligence arrived that on January 27th, 1649: 'He, the said Charles Stuart, as tyrant, traitor, murderer, and public enemy to the good people of this nation, shall be put to death by the severing of his head from his body.'

Lucy watched helplessly as Charles read the sentence numbly, over and over again, not wishing to believe what his eyes saw. Mary retreated to her room and would not see anyone for days.

'That Kingship should amount to a death no better than that of the worst criminals,' said Charles to William. His brother-in-law did not reply. He knew of no words that might comfort Charles in his grief.

It was on the 30th day of January, 1649, one of those days that offers no hope to the human spirit, that Charles I of England walked through his palace at Whitehall for the last time. He had been very fond of St. James's but there was little time left for regrets now. Stepping out into the cold air of the park and Spring Gardens, he was glad he had asked for extra clothing. He would have none believe a coward's soul beat within him; if he shivered, it would be from the cold, not fright.

Eleven years earlier Charles had been able to tell his nephew he was 'the happiest King in Christendom', and so he had been, but he had come to learn that all states pass and beliefs change. But there was one belief that he had always held and on which he would not compromise and that was his belief in the divine right of kings. This principle was dearer than life to him and for this belief he was being led to the scaffold now. He spared one last glance at Inigo Jones's Banqueting House, with the magnificent Ruben's ceiling, then, with great dignity, more kingly than he had ever been in his life, he went to meet his death.

'I pray God my worst fears will not come to pass,' said Charles Stuart to Lucy, in the last days of that cruellest of months, January, 1649.

'If it were within my power, I would grant Parliament any request it might make; I would die in my father's place, renounce the crown, never return to England again — anything, so that his life might be spared.'

Lucy searched her heart, but could find no words to comfort Charles, to dispel the vampires that appeared in the night and left him drenched in his own sweat.

February came, bringing cold winds that swept across the flat lands of Holland, but Charles would have ignored the weather if he could have intelligence his father was safe. In vain did he study the faces of the courtiers in Mary's palace, yet everyone's eyes avoided him. The uncertainty he felt was almost as bad as the fear.

It fell to Lucy to tell Charles what others feared to say. Ann Hill, a maid whose English mistress had suddenly died in The Hague, and who was now employed by Lucy, had a sweetheart, a groom, lately arrived from England.

'Ann, if you know King Charles's fate, then it is your duty

to tell me,' said Lucy. When the girl hesitated, Lucy took her by the arm and shook her.

'Tell me, girl, or I will dismiss you on the spot, and then where will your secrecy land you?' demanded Lucy.

Ann had been afraid to confirm or deny what she had heard, but now felt bound to tell her mistress all that she had been told.

'The King, all agreed who witnessed the execution, was the bravest King in Christendom. Most people in the crowd were sorry for him. My Gavin said London has become a dismal place under Noll Cromwell, he would like to see the . . .'

'Tell me about the King, not what your Gavin thinks about London under the Roundheads,' said Lucy, impatiently.

Ann sulked for a moment, then went on: 'The King held his head high — Oh! Gavin said he was a real King, so dignified, so unafraid. Cromwell had said he would cut the King's head off, crown and all, but Gavin said that when the King was executed the crowd gave a horrible groan that he never wished to hear again.'

Lucy was sickened by what she had heard, but Charles was now King of England, and it was her duty, as a loyal citizen, not just as his mistress, to tell him.

'Lucy, you did right to tell me,' said Charles 'and I will always thank you for not keeping it from me. It was news I would have given my life not to hear, but it was necessary that I should know. My father died a noble death, for his beliefs. A king can be wrong, misguided, but there is nothing finer than to lose one's life defending what one believes to be right.'

Charles spent the rest of the day, and most of the night, with a Protestant priest. He had come to Holland as a youth of eighteen, adventurous and daring, knowing what it was to live the life of a fugitive, to be hunted, to be constantly aware of danger. In the Netherlands he had arrived as a boy and a prince, but now he had become a man and a king. He prayed for the soul of his father, for comfort for his mother, but most of all, he prayed that he would be equal to the burdens that lay ahead of him.

Chapter 6

Henrietta Maria gazed out of the window at the gardens of the Louvre, her heart as frozen as the plants outside. Spring would never return now, for Charles I, the husband who had been dearer than her own life, had been executed and she wished with all her heart that she had died with him.

It was the Earl of St. Albans who broke the news to her. Explaining to the Duchess of Vendôme, whose husband had been a supporter of the king during his struggle with Parliament, why he was going to tell her, the Earl said, 'It is a task I take no pleasure in, rather I would do anything but this. It is cruel to tell her, but crueller far not to.'

But there would have been no need for St. Albans to speak, for the look in his eyes, the pained and compassionate expression on his face, was enough to tell the Queen of the dreaded fate that had befallen her beloved Charles.

'Your Majesty,' began the Earl, but the Queen did not avert her eyes from the window, making no acknowledgement of what he was saying. She remembered that in ancient Greece the bearer of bad news was always killed. When the courtier had finished, Henrietta Maria's face was like a mask. Dismissing him with a curt nod, she sat by the window all day, seeing nothing but Charles mounting the steps to the scaffold, hearing him say, over and over, 'I owe the account of my actions to God alone.'

Lady Morton, Minette's governess, placed food in front of the queen, but she did not look at it. As darkness fell, the

Duchess of Vendôme, the Queen's friend since childhood, entered the room to prepare her for bed. At last, the Queen spoke, 'Perhaps it is true what they say.'

'What do they say, Madame?'

'They whisper behind my back that my husband died because I would not allow him to sacrifice his principles.'

'Your Majesty, that is far from the truth, and no-one says it or thinks it,' said the loyal Vendôme, though she had heard the same sentiments expressed and knew in her heart there was some truth in them.

'What good are principles to the dead? If he had not kept to his principles, he would be alive now,' said the Queen and she began to weep then, all the desperate uncertainties of the last few months that had culminated in savage butchery, on a wooden scaffold, on a cold day in London, pouring out in large tears that sprang from her soul.

Gently, the Duchess gathered her friend into her arms and nursed her like a baby.

'Come now, Madame, you upset yourself over things that cannot be changed. You have suffered greatly, but Your Majesty will know better days.'

'My best days have been, Vendôme, and the light has gone out of my life,' and she began to cry again, even lamenting her need to weep.

'I am a Queen, yet I cry like any peasant.'

'Do not blame yourself, Madame, your loss has been great, but you have your religious faith to comfort you.'

'I find no comfort in anything,' said the Queen, forlornly.

Father Cyprien joined them, but Henrietta Maria was not ready to listen to his words or join him in prayer. In her awful grief, she was inconsolable.

All through that agonising night, the Duchess of Vendôme sat by the Queen's side, mopping her brow with lavender water, holding her hand, reassuring her. Yes, Vendôme was a true friend and glittered like a precious diamond in the dark world that surrounded the Queen.

Henrietta Maria had left her country at the age of fifteen,

to become the child-bride of a stranger in a foreign land. At the time, Vendôme had envied her friend but now, she who had been the Queen of England, aroused only pity and sympathy in her friend's heart.

The Duchess waited with the Queen through that long night.

'Dormez-vous, Madame, dormez-vous?' whispered the Duchess, but sleep did not come to Henrietta Maria, only ghouls prancing out of the walls and dark corners of the room.

'Let me moisten your lips with wine,' but the Queen refused.

'My husband would have drunk nothing before, before . . .' but the words failed to come and she sank back, a broken figure, onto the pillows.

Vendôme went to a cupboard in the far corner of the room. Wisely, she had taken the precaution of obtaining a draught for the night from the apothecary. She poured a measure of the drugs into a wineglass.

'Madame, I have physick here. You cannot refuse this.'

Reluctantly, Henrietta Maria swallowed what she was given. Soon, she fell into a deep sleep, stirring only occasionally to call 'Charles, Charles,' and then she whimpered once or twice, like a baby, and called for her mother, Marie de Medici.

Vendôme replenished the oil lamps and added a few lumps of coal to the fire. The flickering flames were a shield against the night's horrible goblins. She shared her friend's horror, but at a distance, for it had not been her husband's head that had rolled on the scaffold. It had not fallen to her to be royal and, for that, she was grateful.

The next day, Henrietta Maria allowed Father Cyprien to visit her.

'I would fly to Charles this very moment, were I able. His soul would meet mine in eternity. What unimaginable bliss it would be.'

The Queen spoke like a person touched by the certainty

of madness and seeing her demeanour, the faraway look in her eyes, hearing her words, Cyprien de Garnache was deeply troubled for her sanity. She was a woman ruled by her passions and he knew she would go wherever they led her. Every word he uttered now would be very important in influencing her thoughts.

'We owe God a life, Your Majesty. Your life is here, on earth, as long as it pleases God.'

He watched her closely, but did not think his words had any effect on her.

'And then, there is Minette. She needs you.'

Minette was the darling of the Queen's heart and mention of her name brought a flicker to Henrietta Maria's eyes, a softening of her features.

'Charles will need his mother's guiding hand,' continued the priest.

At the mention of Charles's name, the Queen's head gave a little jerk.

The cleric felt a little easier in himself now. By appealing to her strong love for her children, he would be able to bargain with her.

* * *

'King I may be, but a King without teeth, without power, lacking the means to buy even decent mourning clothes, to give my father the respect due to him,' Charles remarked bitterly to Lucy. 'I must leave you a while and go to Paris to comfort my mother.'

Lucy's face showed her disappointment for a moment, but she quickly recovered, for she knew Henrietta Maria's need was greater than her own at that time. She had been expecting Charles to say he was going to visit his mother and it was partly because of his consideration for others that she loved Charles.

'I will return as soon as I can,' he said, taking her in his arms.

'Look after yourself until I am back.'

Without Lucy's company, the Louvre seemed a joyless place to Charles. He could not help remember when he had visited it the last time and Lucy's enthusiasm for Paris had been infectious. Now all he could think of was the grief of his mother. Charles felt her sadness even before he saw her.

'How is my mother? How did she take the news?' asked Charles of the Duchess of Vendôme. He was dressed in sumptuous purple mourning, that William of Orange had given him.

The Duchess shrugged her shoulders and held out her hands in a disconsolate way.

'She loved your father. She is heartbroken and I doubt that she will ever recover, but she will be so glad to see you.'

They entered Henrietta Maria's private apartment, where she was slumped in a chair. Hearing her friend's footsteps, she turned. It was as though she could not believe her eyes when she saw Charles. Leaping to her feet, she threw back her head and opened her arms.

'My boy, my Charles,' she cried, hugging and kissing him with tears flowing down her cheeks at the same time. She was so pleased to see him, but he reminded her so much of her dead husband that it took all her strength to check her tears.

Later, they were joined by Father Cyprien and Lady Morton. Henrietta Maria felt a little stronger now that Charles was with her, but though she wanted to be calm for his sake, yet she could not take her mind off her plight.

'I have had blessings poured upon me in this life, yet I have known the sufferings of Job,' said the Queen. 'I have had everything that any woman could want — a husband who loved me, children, a throne, a country. But what am I left with? Henry and Elizabeth are prisoners in that most cruel of castles, Carisbrooke, Minette and I are unwelcome exiles, penniless, virtually, in my own father's country and you, Charles, are little more than a vagrant. I am indeed La Reigne Malheureuse. That anyone should have suffered as much as I! If it were not for my children, I could wish myself finished with this life.'

She paused for breath and those around her were glad that she had shown some animation. The quiet voice of Father Cyprien was heard then, 'Duty, Madame, duty. You have understood the meaning of the word all your life. You cannot abandon the principle now, especially when your son Charles will need your support.'

All eyes turned and looked at Charles, who inclined his head in agreement.

'Great burdens will fall on your eldest son, and he will bear them more easily with his mother's help.'

Henrietta's heart lifted a little. There was work for her to do in this world, yet. For the sake of her husband, and for the sake of Charles, she would endeavour to be strong.

All the while, Charles said nothing. He had never loved his mother and felt only pity for her now. The merchant classes in England were demanding a share in government, but she was inflexible and bigoted. It was her burning fanaticism that had been the downfall of his father. Charles was a pragmatist, a sailor willing to tack and veer, change course if necessary, to keep the boat afloat. Like his Bourbon grandfather, Henri le Roi, he cultivated a bad memory, which was useful when it came to forgiving one's enemies.

Lady Morton, sitting a little apart from the group, saw the thoughtful expression on Charles's face. She remembered a night, long ago, when her husband had sat with an old crony, staring into the ashes of a dying fire. The subject was the House of Stuart and her husband's words floated down the years to her.

'The family is jinxed. They are descendants of Macbeth and ill-fate will always accompany them.'

Looking at the young Charles, the old governess saw a man possessed of a worldly sophistication that his father had never known. His personality was strong and magnetic, his presence vibrant. He had the confidence born of knowing he could please a woman, she'd wager. Charles I had never been able to impress the ladies, being tongue-tied and quick tempered. Many of his remarks to the Queen's ladies-in-waiting had been of an improper nature, probably, she guessed, in the vain hope of gaining their attention. But he had been a faithful husband and his wife felt her loss grievously. Lady Morton let out a deep sigh. She could only pray that for Charles II, a more peaceful life lay ahead.

* * *

On February 17th, 1649, Charles was proclaimed King by the citizens of Jersey. It was a small victory for Charles, but for the people of Jersey it was an act of high treason, punishable by death.

In The Hague, Lucy heard the news and was quietly jubilant. Although she missed Charles, she was glad to have the last few weeks of her confinement to herself. She had grown very tired and enormously huge. She did not think that her company would have been any fun for him. At the same time, she hoped he was not finding his fun elsewhere. Lucy had a keen understanding of Charles's personality and knew that for him, love was wherever he found it.

Charles had made a carriage available for Lucy and her maid, Ann Hyde, to travel in, whenever they found life indoors too tedious. There was as much food as they needed, and more, but Lucy was thankful when April blossomed and wiped away all traces of winter. It had been a breezy night, but it was not the wind that had kept Lucy awake. When morning dawned, she was in no doubt that it was time to call the midwife. Her pains were bad, though she had drunk the raspberry leaf tea every day. Ann bathed her face with cold water and rubbed her back and then, when Lucy thought she could bear the pain no more, her waters broke and James, the future Duke of Monmouth, entered the world, slippery as a fish, with a face like a boiled dumpling. Lucy was exhausted, but delighted with the child she had brought into the world.

'Will he be called Charles, my Lady?' enquired Ann.

'No, he will be called James, for he comes from a line of Kings,' replied Lucy, taking the baby that had been washed and dried and tightly swaddled.

'Baban bach, cariad Mam, Mother's baby darling,' exulted Lucy. These moments were for her and the new arrival alone.

Ann looked at the baby closely. She was not sure whether he looked like Charles or Colonel Sydney. The midwife whispered that he bore a close resemblance to Sydney, even to the wart on his nose, but she was careful not to say it within Lucy's hearing.

Lucy lay back on the pillows, thankful it was all over and the pain had gone.

She had a son to show Charles when he returned. It would not matter to Charles whose son he was, for he would love them both, such was his nature.

'Ann, I shall not have a wet nurse,' declared Lucy. 'A King's son should be suckled by his mother, not by some poor wretch from the back streets.'

Lucy was in that state of heightened excitement that accompanies the birth of a child. She saw a golden future lying ahead of her baby boy, a world where honours and glory would be heaped on the head that was now bald as a coot's, save for a whisp of dark hair. If a soothsayer had been present he might have warned the mother that grave dangers lay ahead, obstacles would be put in the path of her new-born son and he would have many enemies only too eager to plot his downfall. But Lucy would not have wanted to be told anything like that. As far as she was concerned, one day her boy might be King of England.

In the Convent of the Carmelites in Paris, Henrietta Maria was reading the Deus Misereatur, when news was brought to her that Lucy had borne a son.

'Have I not suffered enough?' she demanded of Father Cyprien.

'That my son, a King, should dally with this Lucy Walter.

It is more than I should have to bear. To think that a King's child — if it is a King's child, and from reports reaching me I am beginning to doubt that it is Charles's child, to think that a King's child should be born the wrong side of the sheets. Oh, I know he loves this Lucy in his way, but he could love La Grande Mademoiselle as well as this Welsh girl, and Mademoiselle has the biggest fortune in Europe to recommend her. He could love my niece if he put his mind to it.'

She paused for breath: 'Even if he married her and found he could not love her, he would still have her fortune to console him.'

The priest was aware of that strange mixture of spirituality and worldliness that composed her nature. Although her mind was on the next world for much of the time, yet she was determined that while she was still here on earth, she would see her son Charles sitting on the English throne.

Minette was happy to hear that her brother Charles now had a son.

'Perhaps it will occupy Mamma's thoughts for a while and help her to forget that she wants me to marry Louis,' whispered the little girl to Lady Morton.

As far as Minette cared, La Grande Mademoiselle could have Louis; she wanted to please Mamma, but she did not want to marry a boy, albeit the King of France, in whom she had no interest.

Whilst Lucy was oblivious to the goings on of the outside world, so wrapt up was she in the care and nursing of her darling Jamie, Charles did not find that his new role as a father had in any way dampened his ardour. Indeed, his separation from Lucy had merely served to rekindle his amorous nature. Looking around for a suitable recipient for his affections, his eyes alighted on his first cousin, Sophie, the daughter of his gay Aunt Elizabeth, Queen of Bohemia, with whom he soon resumed his acquaintanceship.

It was one of those soft, early summer nights, when Charles had managed to coax his cousin to take a stroll along the promenade with him. Carried away by the beauty of the night, the fresh charms of his cousin and his own impetuousness, Charles decided to make no bones about the matter, but to come straight to the point, and speak his mind to Sophie.

'I could love you far more than Lucy Walter,' he declared boldly. This statement did not have the desired effect on his cousin, who was not in the least pleased. Fond as Sophie was of Charles, she did not see a man with a wife and baby as a possible suitor for herself. The only way out of what, for her, was a tricky situation, was to plead a corn on her little toe, which she did, thus necessitating a hasty end to what Charles had thought was going to be a romantic interlude.

Later, recalling the incident to his brother James, Charles chuckled.

'Our cousin Sophie is a somewhat naïve child, let me warn you. I expect she thought I had taken her out to admire the milky way, and for no other reason.'

James listened gravely. Charles was a man of the world, and he deeply admired his brother. James wanted to be like Charles. Their mother complained about Charles's way with women, but Charles was alright. Women liked him. He knew how to treat a woman. James would make sure he had women everywhere he went, too.

Soon after this, Charles left for Jersey. Henrietta Maria missed him when he had gone and spoke wistfully of him to her niece, La Grande Mademoiselle.

'Every woman in Europe has set her heart on my Charles. He is the King of a great nation. It is only time before he will be restored to his throne.'

'But will he be restored? That is the question,' said that impertinent Mademoiselle.

Her aunt found La Grande Mademoiselle so trying. She had a way of asking the most infuriating questions. It was almost impossible to have a reasonable conversation with her, especially now that Mademoiselle had proven herself to be the heroine of the Frondeurs.

Why, here she was, promised to Louis XIV, and openly opposing his mother and her lover, Cardinal Mazarin, by having supported the wars of the Fronde. Henrietta Maria could not understand the girl.

She was no great beauty by any standards; her over-large nose had seen to that, but she possessed a glow of triumph, which came from having been the toast of the street-fighters. She also had an air of contempt about her, which came from her belief that she was better than others. When she began speaking again, her aunt looked at her suspiciously.

'Besides, your Charles has a mistress and a baby, too, which he openly acknowledges. Is that the proper way for a King to behave?'

Henrietta Maria snorted with impatience. This girl knew how to rile her.

'Charles is a proper man. What if he does have a mistress? My father had many mistresses. Did he love my mother any the less? Was he less a King because of it? Do you want a man or a mouse for a husband?'

La Grande Mademoiselle was silent for once. She was as good as any man, the wars of the Fronde had shown everyone she could stand her ground as well as the next man, and better than most. What use did a woman like her have for a man, especially a man who could not keep his mind off wenching for long. No, she could do better for herself than throw herself away on her cousin, Charles Stuart. She would resist her father's attempts to marry her to Louis, King of France, though he had been promised to her since he was a baby. And a mere baby he would always be, compared to her, and compared to Condé. For Condé had proved himself a brilliant soldier in the wars of the Fronde and had crushed the Spanish armies under his heel at Rocroi. Prince of France he was by birth, but a prince among soldiers he had proved himself to be. Yes, it was only Condé who was a fit husband for her, a man who could fight pitilessly, a man driven by blood and iron, who showed no mercy, who had no regrets, a man who did not hesitate to do what had to be done. Everyone else was a pale shadow compared to him and could rouse no passion, only scorn, in La Grande Mademoiselle. There was ony one small obstacle that stood between her and marriage to Condé and that was his wife, still, c'est la vie.

Charles returned from Jersey to find motherhood suited Lucy very well.

'Charles, here is your Jamie,' said Lucy, placing the gurgling baby in the King's arms. 'Everyone says he is like you and will be a great soldier when he is a man.'

'Ah, Lucy, I hope I will have won my throne back long before Jamie grows up, so that he will never know the struggles his father had in the battlefield.'

The baby whimpered and Lucy took him from Charles. Undoing the bodice of her dress, she settled back to suckle the child. Pushing her pink nipple into the baby's mouth he stopped crying and, with a contented sigh, suckled hungrily, the milk leaking out from the corner of his mouth and dripping down his chin. Charles put his arms around Lucy and Jamie; he loved them both so much. Why had he been away so long, when all this was waiting for him here?

When Jamie had taken all he could, he regurgitated a mouthful of milk over Charles's hand. The King laughed, licked the milk off his hand and said, 'I understand now why he enjoys it so much.'

Watching Lucy bathing the infant, Charles knew he could so easily lose himself in the ecstasy of this small world, which consisted of just the three of them.

'I can see that Jamie is the apple of his mother's eye. It is a good thing that I returned when I did, else Jamie would have supplanted me in your affections,' said Charles with a chuckle.

Lucy marvelled at Charles's good spirits. He had accepted Jamie as his own without question and despite all the troubles of the past months, he had not lost any of his sense of humour. That night, in bed, Lucy was pleased to find that Charles had not lost any of his desire for her, either. She had wondered, in his absence, if there had been other women and she was almost certain there had been, but his ardour for her was still the same as ever.

Charles was ready to slip into a state of domestic bliss, but news came that the dissenters in Scotland were ready to crown him King in Scone.

'Why do you hesitate?' asked Lucy. 'To be crowned in Scotland will give you a backdoor into England. Take the chance while you have it.'

'Lucy, you do not understand the issues involved. My father's titles included that of Defender of the Faith and the Church of Scotland is against the Church of England.'

Charles was learning that the state of kingship was often a solitary calling. Lucy had a simplistic view of most matters; Henrietta Maria had no patience with the Covenanters as their avowed aim was to destroy Popery and if there was one lesson Charles had learnt from his father's mistakes, it was that an inflexible disposition and rigid intellect could spell downfall.

His mind went back to a letter his father had sent him, when he was a young boy under the tutellage of Peter Massonet.

'I would not have you too studious, for too much contemplation spoils action . . . Wherefore take heed of too much book.'

Well, thought Charles ruefully, there had never been any fear of his being too fond of his books, yet those who loved him knew he was not a thoughtless man.

In the end, it was the precept of his maternal grandfather, Henri of Navarre, Henri Quatre, that decided him. King Henri had learnt that to keep the Bourbons on the throne of France it had been necessary to change his religion. He had explained it by saying: 'Paris is worth a mass,' and, said like that, it did not seem too awful a thing to compromise one's religious beliefs when expediency and the tide of fortune demanded it. Why, George Villiers, son of his father's favourite, and a man in whose judgement Charles had implicit faith, was urging him to sign the Covenant that the Scots were offering him. Although there were those who said that nothing in heaven or earth was sacred to Villiers, yet Charles was inclined to think Villiers's judgement was right in this matter. Yes, he, Charles would come to an agreement with the Scots and, later, he would tackle the problem of the Church of England. Doubtless, there were those who would accuse him of taking the easy way out, but there was no easy way to regain the English throne.

At the Louvre, Henrietta Maria felt only anguish in what she saw as Charles's collusion with the Scots.

'Have I not suffered too much already?' she demanded of the Duchess of Vendôme. 'I have prayed to the Virgin and all the saints in heaven that Charles would change his mind and not go to Scotland. Does he ever stop to ask his mother's advice? I can hear the cry of the Scots even now, and always it is the same — No Popery, no Popery! It is a cry that will follow me to my grave and beyond.'

But then the queen heard that Charles had made up his mind he was going to Scotland and refused to change it, despite his mother's entreaties.

How like Charles to listen to all the wrong people. She could see Villiers, the boy her husband had looked after like his own, at Charles's elbow, ingratiating himself into Charles's confidence, urging him on to recklessness. What did they used to say of Villiers? She searched her mind to remember. Ah! that was it — a man wholly given to mirth and pleasure. Well, that was not a charge that could be levelled against Charles, for he had already suffered too much for the sake of kingship.

At The Hague, Charles concluded the details with the Marquis of Montrose.

'Fear not, I shall give you every power to act in my name, Sir,' said Charles. 'In my name, you shall march into England any time you choose.'

'If it takes force to restore Your Majesty to the throne,

then all the might of the Scottish army will do it,' said the brave Marquis.

If it grieved Charles to perform the oath, he did not show any emotion.

The pledge of a Stuart might be slight, but Charles felt the greatest grief at having to take his leave of Jamie and Lucy. It took all his will power to leave his nut-brown mistress and her chuckling baby boy.

'I shall be gone before long, Lucy, but never from your thoughts, I trust.'

'I will be true to you as any wife could ever be,' said Lucy passionately.

'My Black Boy will always be in my thoughts and heart,' she said, giving him the tenderest of kisses.

Charles was enough of a realist to accept that Lucy's constancy was not a thing to be relied on, yet with Jamie's arrival he had hoped that some of her restless nature had been quelled. Locked in Lucy's embrace, the sweet smell of her body in his nostrils, he found no pleasure in the thought of returning to the company of men, their unclean ways, their crude oaths, their rough way of life. He would rather stay with Lucy, feel her skin against his at night, smooth and fragrant as a nectarine's. Perhaps one day he would be restored to his throne, married to some boring sprig of European royalty, surrounded by powdered and pampered mistresses. For solace, he would remember these days and nights with Lucy and Jamie and think that a king can be as happy as any man in the land if he has his memories.

* * *

Charles had been gone for only a matter of weeks, before Lucy was restless. One morning, she insisted on going to the market to buy provisions, taking Ann Hill with her.

'We will not be away long and Jamie will be perfectly content with Angelique,' said Lucy, referring to one of the maids.

Ann did not think it seemly that her mistress should go marketing, but once Lucy had made up her mind, she could not be dissuaded.

When their basket was full, they set off for home.

'I think it best that we do not return by the bridle path, ma'am,' said the maid.

'Why ever not? I prefer to go that way. Come,' commanded Lucy firmly. 'It will make a change and the air will do us good.'

Reluctantly, the maid followed her mistress. In the market she had noticed a man watching them closely, but if she mentioned it to Lucy she would only laugh at her fears.

A rider passed by and doffed his hat in greeting to the two women.

'There now, admit it. You are enjoying this walk,' said Lucy. 'I do not know why you made so much fuss in the beginning. It is a long time since I have been away from the city, even for a short while.'

Lucy's enjoyment was so evident that Ann began to share her enthusiasm.

It was just then that Ann heard what sounded like a twig snapping, yet there did not appear to be anyone else around, so perhaps it was a bird dropping a twig, or even her imagination. But before Ann had time to ponder further, a man appeared from the undergrowth. It was the man she had seen earlier in the market, the man who had been watching them so closely, the man with eyes dark and brown as the liver she had fed the cat that morning. The maid felt a streak of fear, swift as lightning, dart through her body, paralyzing her movement, silencing the cry of warning on her lips. Lucy was not aware of his presence, but with one leap, he darted forward, grabbing Lucy from behind, pulling her hair roughly until her head jerked back and she screamed out in terror.

Ann ran forward to help her mistress, but he dealt her a glancing blow across the cheek, so that she crumbled onto the ground. Lucy was stronger than Ann and struggled with the ruffian, but he pulled her to the ground by her hair. As he came down on Lucy, rancid breath assailed her nostrils and a rough hand came round her neck, squeezing it until she was coughing and gasping for air. Lucy felt she was going to pass out, but she was vaguely aware that the man was saying something in Walloon, a language she did not speak, but she knew what he wanted, and it was money. Money first, anyway, and she could not bear to think what else then. Lucy began to fumble for her purse and as soon as she found it, the man snatched it from her and tore it open. With a muttered curse, he realised there were only a few coins left. Fear overcame Lucy and she began screaming hysterically.

This infuriated the rogue, who stuck his fingers down her throat.

Lucy believed she had breathed her last gasp, when a horse's hooves were heard, thudding heavily down the path. This surprised the attacker, who immediately made to get away.

'Not so fast, my man,' said an English voice.

The rider hastily dismounted and kneed the man in the groin, then for good measure, knocked him senseless.

Sir Henry Bennett knelt down by Lucy and pressed a flask of brandy to her lips.

'You poor, poor thing,' he said. 'The rogue deserves hanging for what he has done to you.'

Lucy was badly shaken, but realised her rescuer was English, and a gentleman.

As she lay recovering on the ground, Ann stirred.

'Mistress, I told you not to come this way,' was the first thing Ann could say.

'I know,' said Lucy. 'It was my own fault and I am sorry. But how lucky we have been, Ann, to be rescued by . . .'

'Henry Bennett, ma'am. Please do not thank me, but save your strength.'

Placing Lucy on the horse and assisting Ann as best he could, Henry Bennet, the future Earl of Arlington, helped the two women home.

It took many days for Lucy to recover from her ordeal.

'What will His Majesty say when he hears about this?' speculated Ann.

'He is not to hear a word about that unfortunate incident, do you hear?' demanded Lucy sharply. 'And he is not to be told anything about Sir Henry, either. You breathe a word, and I will dismiss you.'

Ann sighed. Lucy could be so sharp tongued. Ann had warned her not to accept the attention and flattery of their rescuer but, in this, as in all other things, Lucy would not be told.

If Lucy had missed Charles, she soon forgot about his absence in the arms of Sir Henry Bennett. For Lucy, the man in her arms, the lover in her bed, was always of more importance than any previous commitment. When she paused to think of Charles which was not often, she imagined that he had other consolations while he was away from her. And, there could be no denying, a Cavalier and a Colonel, like Henry Bennett, gave Lucy adequate compensation for not having Charles's company. In her quieter moments, she reflected that only Charles had the magic, no one inflamed her passions like Charles, no one could stride into the room, throw her on the bed and love her till her senses spun and the world was transformed into a magical paradise, like Charles could. Did he find all other women inadequate? Or was the thrill of the chase, and not what came after, the thing that mattered most for him? She would never know.

* * *

'Who knows what the outcome of his time in Scotland will be?' said Lucy to Ann Hill one day. 'Perhaps the dour Scots, who seem to have such a hold over him, will also choose his bride for him. For all I know La Grande Mademoiselle may tire of her role as Joan of Arc in the street fighting in Paris and choose to throw her great fortune in Charles's lap. Who could say no to a dowry of those proportions? Or some other fine lady may come along and claim Charles as her prize and I may never see him again. Am I to sit here, twiddling my thumbs till my hair turns grey and my teeth drop out, when there are other comforts on offer to me?'

'You could try a little patience, ma'am,' ventured the maid.

'When I want your opinion, I shall ask for it,' said Lucy, curtly.

In a softer voice, she said, 'No, Ann, I would be a fool to myself if I believed Charles would ever make me his wife. Why, half the eligible daughters of Europe's leading families are setting their bait for him. When a King marries, it is not for love, but for expediency, to strengthen his throne and the position of his country.' She turned, and gazed at the garden, frilled with the gaudy flowers of high summer. When she spoke, her voice was quiet and wistful.

'I could give my heart to Charles, and him alone, but I know it can never be. The best I can hope for is to be his favourite mistress, if he returns. I shall never forget what we had, but the only hold I have over him is the memories we share.'

* * *

Charles arrived in Scotland accompanied by a Dutch fleet, a raggle taggle Court and George Villiers. He was given a rapturous welcome and a pension of nine thousand pounds a month, which did not leave much room to manoeuvre once all the hangers-on had been paid.

In Scotland, Charles was to learn that every day of the week resembled a Sunday. One sermon was so long that the curate, in weariness, constantly wiped his face with his black leather gloves. By the time the sermon ended, the man's face was black as coal and George Villiers laughed uncontrollably. If the sermons were lengthy, the prayers were even longer. This sort of piety was not to the King's liking and he was moved to say to his father's friend, Lauderdale, 'Let Presbytery go! 'Tis no religion for a gentleman.'

More than a year passed, a time when Charles learnt that the firmest promises, the gallantest deeds, have the habit of turning to ash overnight. He had gone to Scotland in the hope of defeating Cromwell and marching victoriously into England. At Worcester the defeat he suffered would have crushed the spirit of a lesser man, but Charles was thankful to escape to the Continent with his life intact. After Worcester there were those who said that Charles's gaiety was not as apparent as before.

Whilst Charles could accept defeat in war, it was harder when it came to love.

'I do not deny that I have had my diversions, what man would not have?' he remarked to Villiers, 'but I did not expect Lucy to forget me so quickly. To have borne Bennett's child . . .'

Lucy pleaded with Charles to overlook what she called her 'little lapse'.

'We will pretend you have not been away and you are the father of little Mary. Please, Charles, my Black Boy,' she said in her wheedling tone, putting her arms around his neck.

But it was too late for Lucy, and Charles moved abruptly away from her.

'Lucy, this is not fairyland. Be realistic.'

When Charles had recovered his pride he decided that, perhaps, it was to his advantage that Lucy had transferred her affection to another man.

When he regained his throne, it was inevitable he would seek a suitable bride. The longer he was with Lucy, the harder it would have been for him to break with her. And there were other things to think of now, besides his pride.

* * *

The wars of the Fronde were over. Never again would Louis XIV be blackmailed by powerful nobles who controlled their private armies from their provincial estates. The days of civil war were gone and Louis did not want to witness the spectacle of Frenchmen fighting each other again, as he had at the battle of Fauborg St. Antoine.

As he headed the triumphant procession that rode into Paris, the city that was his by right, the city that was now lined up to cheer his glittering retinue, Louis found comfort in the belief he held so dearly, 'God governs all.'

At Louis's side was his cousin, King Charles II of England and close to them rode the loyal Duc de Vendôme, bastard son of their grandfather, Henri IV of France and Navarre.

This was a wonderful day for Louis, for France, for la gloire and most of all, for Anne of Austria, his mother, dressed in cloth of gold and sparkling with jewels, waving from her carriage. Louis, le Dieu Donne, God's gift to her in her old age, the boy who had been called 'beautiful as an angel' and who would be known as 'le Roi Soleil', the Sun King, riding in triumph at the head of a procession that included princes of the blood royal, all the noble families, known as le grand, officers of the Crown, the Excise, Parlement, professors and doctors of the Sorbonne, gorgeous in their gowns and hoods, the merchants of the guilds and the household troops with the sound of the horses hooves and tack ringing out like the notes of an exquisite Te Deum, sung by an angelic choir — Oh! it was like a dream come true for her.

Looking at Louis and his cousin Charles, Anne could not help thinking how close in temperament they were. Louis had been closely influenced by the plays of Corneille, finding his own parallels with their themes: the struggle between a man's private inclinations and the demands of the state, a man's own sense of civility and integrity and the demands of the country for la gloire. But they had been lucky, for Louise had Mazarin to guide him. It was Mazarin who taught Louis that a king must always put the state first.

Louis had called Mazarin 'le Grand Turk' when he and Anne were together, and she had rebuked her son for it; manners were important for all men, especially a King. Anne did not know it then, but thanks to her early lessons, Louis would become known as 'the politest king in Europe'. And it was Mazarin who had taught Louis to read foreign communiques, how to draft replies to them, how to deal with state papers.

Anne was shrewd enough to know her son hated the Cardinal for insisting he learnt the business of kingship, but the day would come, after Mazarin's death, when secretaries of state would enquire of Louis, 'From whom do we take our orders and instructions now?' and the King would answer confidently, 'From me.'

Henrietta Maria watched her sister-in-law. Oh! she could see this was a happy day for her, her eldest son the King of France, her second son the Monsieur. No wonder her fat jowls quivered with a deeper ecstasy than any she had experienced with the hateful Mazarin, the Cardinal with the liquid gold eyes and the modulated voice, soft and silky as old brandy when it caresses the throat. Paris, the city so used to l'amour, was buzzing with the scandal of the ageing Queen and her priestly lover. It was an improbable liaison, but if Anne wished to make a fool of herself . . .

Henrietta Maria was human enough to feel some sympathy for Anne, who had known little happiness with her bad-tempered husband. Who could tell if there was any truth in the gossip? On being pressed by a friend to reveal the nature of the relationship, Anne was noncommital, 'I admit I like him and feel tender towards him, but my affection does not amount to love.'

Henrietta Maria could not condemn Anne. She understood too well the demands of the flesh, try to suppress them as she might. In her exile, she had sorely missed Charles, yet even while he was a prisoner in Carisbrooke Castle, she had found comfort in the arms of St. Albans.

The English Queen turned her attention to Philippe, the

boy condemned to be second best to his brother all his life. Poor Philippe, yet he had a quick understanding, a caustic wit and a tongue as sharp as a woman's. One day he would be a soldier so brilliant that his brother would feel the need to justify the reasons why Kings were unable to risk their lives and cover themselves in la gloire. The two cousins, Charles and Louis, were more alike than the two brothers, Louis and Philippe, reflected Henrietta Maria. What was it about Philippe that was so different from the other two, pondered the Queen. Was he too fond of dressing up as a girl, a little too careful with his clothes and appearance?

Henrietta Maria's eyes came to rest now on her niece, La Grande Mademoiselle, who had disgraced herself during the wars of the Fronde. Her reputation was utterly tarnished, but her fortune remained as large as ever. She was no fit wife for her cousin Louis, but her money could help Charles regain the throne of England. Marriage to Charles would also solve the problems of Gaston, Duc d'Orleans, Mademoiselle's father and Henrietta Maria's brother. However blinkered and unimaginative he might be, even he could no longer pretend his daughter had any hopes of marrying the King of France. Besides, Anne of Austria had put up with enough insults from Mademoiselle. No, Minette would make an ideal wife for Louis — her French was perfect, as was her English; she was well versed in the Catholic faith and a sweeter, more compliant wife a man could not hope for. Admittedly, she had no dowry but, in this life, one could not have everything, and besides, Minette's other attractions overcame the lack of a fortune.

And then there was Charles, her beautiful, ugly Charles, riding into Paris with his fourteen year old cousin, Louis. Henrietta Maria breathed a little more easily now that he was rid of the Welsh woman, Lucy Walter.

There was something about the relationship with Lucy that the Queen had feared. She had known, as a mother knows, that it was more than a passing fancy that they had experienced for each other. Whatever it was, it was over now and she hoped Charles had learnt something from it. If a mother's influence counted for anything, then she would see that Minette and Charles made brilliant marriages.

* * *

'Oh, Ann, listen to this!'

Lucy was excitedly reading a letter, newly arrived form London. She did not receive much correspondence, so any letter was bound to be a source of excitement.

'It's from Justus.'

Lucy's cheeks were flushed.

'Justus says that Parliament has requested that the Marriage Register of Saint Thomas a Beckett Church, Haverfordwest, be sent to London, the reason being that Cromwell is determined to find out if, and when, the King and I were married.'

Lucy looked at her maid to see what effect her words had had on her. Ann was too dumbfounded to say anything for a moment. Her thoughts whirled in her head. Perhaps she had misjudged her mistress, perhaps she was not Mistress Barlow, as she liked to style herself, but really Queen Lucy of England. Had 'Mistress Barlow' really been a cover for the fact that she was the wife of Charles Stuart? Had Lucy wanted to confuse her enemies? Ann recovered herself sufficiently to say, 'And were you married, my lady?'

Flushed and agitated as she was, Lucy had no intention of revealing everything to Ann.

'That is none of your business, Ann. You may return to your work now.'

Those who knew Lucy well realised she had an appreciation of when it was best to speak and when it was more judicious to keep quiet. As soon as she had read the letter, Lucy immediately decided that if there were sections of society who believed she was the wife of Charles II, then in no way would she shake that conviction. The assumption might be to her advantage; it certainly could not be to her disadvantage.

Chapter 7

'Ann, brew me another broth of tansy and make it stronger this time.'

There was a note of desperation in Lucy's voice and the maid's lips curled.

'How is your cold, my lady?' she asked, feigning innocence.

'It is no better, but if you make that soup strong, it may improve by tomorrow.'

Out in the herb garden, the maid cut a large swathe of the plant. It was no good her mistress trying to fool her. Cold, indeed. She knew what the draught of tansy was for. Lucy was with child again and it was a condition she wanted to end as soon as possible. Last week it had been castor oil purges and hot baths, now it was the tansy. Her mistress had been consulting that old Welsh book again, written by the physicians of Myddfai. The maid understood now why Lucy had been in a bad humour lately, but she had no sympathy for her. The King had hardly turned his back before Lucy had taken Henry Bennett into her bed and, now, it was not him only. Other women would have played a game of patience until their men returned but for Lucy, that would have been impossible.

'It is maddening the number of different men who call and disturb the peace of the night,' complained Ann to the kitchen maid. 'I do my best to protect the children, so that they do not see the comings and goings. The King himself is back and fore occasionally, too. I am positive it is him I have seen calling. He must be mighty fond of her after all that has happened.'

The next day, Lucy kept to her bed, but the day following that, she rose and, though looking pallid, seemed in better spirits.

'Evidently my tansy portion worked,' laughed Ann, maliciously, to the cook.

In her bedroom, Lucy stretched languorously, raising her arms high above her head, pushing her shoulders back till her breasts stood away from her body. She felt a lot better now that she was free of the burden that had rested inside her like a lump of heavy lead. She ran her hands over her body, rippling the butter-plump flesh. Men could take their pleasures, and women, too, but always there was a price to pay for it. She yawned luxuriously, like a cat, opening her mouth wide, revealing a little pink tongue, sharp white teeth. Her figure was spreading, but she popped a slice of sucket into her mouth. It was hard to give up her treats and she would never give up love, for it was the most delicious pleasure of all. It did not matter if she was a little too plump, for she still looked as soft, sweet and sensuous as a Pembrokeshire milkmaid. That was a part of her charm and that was why half the Cavaliers in Rotterdam found their way to her bed.

Lucy had an idea that the shrieks of laughter in the night, the long silences and the ecstatic groans irritated Ann, but Lucy had no shame, only insatiable desires. The last time she had been with Charles, it was as good as it had always been.

'Do you miss me like you used to?' Lucy could not help asking.

'I miss you all the time.'

'And do you still love me, my Black Boy?'

'I have never stopped loving you and I always will.'

Lucy chose to believe him, though other arms guided his hips to theirs now, lips that were not hers whispered secrets in his ears and when passion was spent, it was to other bodies he was fused in the after glow, but Lucy had no time for regrets. She understood that when Charles loved, he believed it was for ever; at the time he meant it, but the next day he hardly remembered whose arms he had spent the night before in. One woman could not possess him. It was not that he was shallow, but that he had lived with insecurity. Things changed, people changed, love changed. It was as simple as that.

In August a messenger came with a letter for Lucy, written by the King's aide.

'I am to inform you that His Majesty, King Charles II, is ill of a fever. Those who attend him hold little hope for his recovery.'

Lucy's face crumbled. Blackness swirled around her and she thought she might collapse. If Charles were to die . . . She could not bear the thought of it. She willed him to get better.

'Ann, you must remember His Majesty in your prayers, night and morning. He is gravely ill. Oh, if Jamie's father were to die . . .'

Lucy sobbed quietly for a while and Ann felt sorry for her imperious mistress. Lucy was not a person it was easy to feel sorry for, bent on her own pleasures as she always was, but the maid servant knew that her pain was real enough this time.

But Charles did not die. By September he had made a partial recovery and October saw him recuperating in Chantilly. December found him in Paris, where the charms of the ladies were so irresistible, the vices so unavoidable, that he soon found his strength again.

Lucy, too, found ways of speeding the dreary days of winter on their way. It was a while now since she ordered a new dress for herself, but a lovely robe would bring a cheer to the dark days.

'What colour do you think suits me best, Ann?' said Lucy thoughtfully one day, as she sat in front of the looking-glass.

'Come and brush my hair, Ann, and tell me what you think.'

Ann was too wise to advise Lucy, for she knew whatever she said, Lucy would have her own way. Lucy handed the maid some pink, satin ribbons to tie up her ringlets. They were too young for a matron with two little children, but Ann held her tongue. Lucy viewed her reflection with satisfaction. Yes, she could still hold her own with the prettiest girl in town.

'Send for the dressmaker, Ann. Tell her I wish to see some rose-pink stuff. I shall have a dress covered with ribbons and bows.'

A woollen gown in a drab colour would have been more serviceable for the cold winds that blew accross the Netherlands in the winter, but Lucy had no intention of venturing outside her boudoir in the gown and when she entertained her gentlemen callers, the gown would be whisked off in a trice, anyway.

Lucy was in high excitement the next day.

'Ann, make sure the house is shining! I have the most exciting news! His Majesty's resident in Brussels, Sir Henry de Vic, is calling to pay his respects in a day or two. I must have the house filled with flowers, more food, great log fires. And Ann, go round to the dressmaker straight away and tell her I will pay her more if she finishes that dress quickly. And tell her not to forget I want the bodice deeply cut.'

Ann sighed wearily. Another man for Lucy to beguile. It seemed the whole world was full of men, seeking out Mistress Walter for their satisfaction.

When Sir Henry de Vic arrived at Lucy's modest house in Rotterdam, he was charmed by what he saw. He had heard that the lady was comely, and so she was, but he had not been told about her exuberant personality, which he found utterly charming. Soon they were chatting together as though they had known each other all their lives, and not a matter of hours.

'Ann, you will put the children to bed early tonight, and go to bed yourself as soon as you are ready.'

Ann knew what that meant. Sir Henry was an old man but there was no fool like an old fool.

Sir Henry felt inside his pocket for the present he had brought Lucy.

'May I present a small gift?' he enquired, handing Lucy the little box.

Lucy squealed delightedly and her glee was infectious.

She held the ear-rings up to the light, the two amber beads glistening in the glow of the candles. For a brief moment they reminded Lucy of the necklace Sir Richard had given her all those years ago.

'Oh, you naughty man, spoiling me like this,' said Lucy.

He was fifty four and she was treating him like a schoolboy and he loved it. She pressed her full lips against his and he was utterly enchanted.

Lucy held the jewels up to the light once more, then dropped them down the low cut bodice of the rose-pink, satin dress.

'Now look what you made me do,' she laughed coquettishly, 'I have lost them and you will have to find them.'

Lucy played the most exciting games. Before long, she thought of other places, equally delightful, to 'lose' the earrings. Rapturously, Sir Henry took his time in finding them. Lucy, realising Sir Henry's passions were easily satisfied, pressed his face into her lovely breasts, planted kisses on top of his bald plate and tickled his ear lobes with her plump fingers, until he thought he had found paradise on earth. They romped and frolicked the night away and the grateful old gentleman declared he had never known such ecstasies; he felt like a lad with his first lass, but happier. He had not expected such a harvest of contentment in his old age.

All night long, Lucy thought of new games to play, but when dawn broke, Sir Henry had the best idea of all: they would get married and this divine state of affairs could go on for ever! This was endless joy, bliss, and the besotted man was ecstatic. Mistress Barlow was everything he had been led to believe, and more. He was in raptures, for the beautiful Lucy had agreed to become his wife! All that was necessary now, was to ask the King's permission for the wedding to proceed.

The next day, Lucy and Sir Henry left for Cologne.

'Wave goodbye to your mother, Jamie,' said Ann, as the carriage rattled away.

'Shush, shush, Mary, do not cry, my little love. Mamma will not be gone long. Come, we will go to find your comforter and Jamie will play peek-a-boo with you.'

Lucy and Sir Henry became the laughing stock of the Continent. News of their mission reached the ears of Elizabeth of Bohemia, Charles's aunt. She found the situation hilarious and wasted no time in writing to Sir Edward Nicholas.

'Sure it is a doting time for King Charles's old ministers of state! I thank God your wife is still alive, for fear you should fall in love again! I am sorry for poor Sir Harry de Vic, as, let the match break or go on, it is every way ill for him.'

Talking to Mary of Orange, Elizabeth said, 'This is the funniest thing I have heard in years. I am not surprised Lucy Barlow wishes to marry a rich man. They may decide to breed . . .' but she failed to finish the sentence, the tears were streaming down her face and her sides were aching from laughter.

The Princess of Orange listened in silence. She did not share her aunt's amusement, seeing Lucy's actions as more of a tragedy than a comedy.

Mary remembered how she had welcomed Lucy as though she had been Charles's wife,sensing that what they felt for each other was more than passing attraction. When Henrietta Maria had railed against Lucy, Mary had taken her part, knowing she brought comfort to Charles after their father's death, but that was in the past, for Lucy had betrayed Charles. Had not she hurt Charles sufficiently with Sir Henry Bennett, without making a spectacle of herself again with Sir Henry de Vic?

'Charles continues to see Lucy occasionally,' remarked Mary, when her aunt's mirth had subsided a little. 'He is still very fond of her.'

'Then he is a fool. He should know by now what sort of a woman she is.'

'She has this hold over him,' replied Mary slowly. 'It is as though he has no will of his own. He acknowledges the boy as his own and while Lucy has the boy, she will always manipulate him.'

'He'll see her for what she is, one day,' said Elizabeth, comfortingly, as she whistled the dogs outside for their walk. The Stuart gayness, so lacking in Charles I, had manifested itself most noticeably in Elizabeth and her nephew, Charles II.

Mary sat thoughtfully for a long while after her aunt's departure. If Charles could not save himself from Lucy, then perhaps she could. It would need careful planning, but there were ways and means and there were those who would be only too pleased to help her . . . people like Tom Howard.

In Cologne, Charles, like Mary, failed to see the joke.

'Charles, dear Charles, don't you see that a comfortable marriage to Sir Henry would benefit Jamie and Mary. Sir Henry will not live forever, but he would leave provision for myself and the children, so that we would not know want.'

'The children do not know want now, and neither do you. There are times when you are impertinent and ungrateful, madam.'

'I did not mean to upset you, Charles, I was only thinking of what was for the best.'

'My answer is still no, Lucy, and I will not discuss the subject any further.'

It needed only a sharp word from the King to put an end to Sir Henry's amorous feelings and he quickly returned to

Brussels, where it was noticed he was careful not to mention the name of Mistress Lucy Barlow again.

Lucy returned to Rotterdam and refused to discuss the subject of Sir Henry with Ann, though Ann was dying to know the details.

'Mamma had to go away for a few days to see your Papa, Jamie, and he is sending you and Mary his love.'

Further information she would not disclose but Ann concluded that whatever had transpired between Lucy, Sir Henry and the King, had not diminished Lucy's appetite for the opposite sex, for soon there was the usual stream of nocturnal visitors and life returned to its normal pattern.

It was not long before Charles forgot his anger over Lucy's request to marry Sir Henry de Vic. Talking to his boon companion, George Villiers, Charles told him he would be out of Cologne for a while and could be found in Rotterdam if Villiers needed to contact him.

'I'll ask no questions as to whom you will be visiting,' said Villiers, with a knowing look.

'Not if you know what is best for you,' said Charles lightheartedly. Even Charles found Villiers trying at times. He would be glad to be away from his company for a while, especially now that he was hearing it said that Villiers might be in the pay of Cromwell. At first, Charles had dismissed the rumours, but now he viewed his friend with mild suspicion, though he found it hard to believe that Villiers, who loved fun as much as he, would be prepared to inform on him. Before Charles left for Rotterdam, he was careful to pack the pearl necklace given him by Henrietta Maria. Holding the beads up to the light, Charles admired their even roundness, their lustrous glow. They would please Lucy, for she loved baubles. If she were ever desperate for money, then she could sell the pearls for a high price. He wanted her to have some security for there might be times when he could not provide for her.

Lucy had no prior information that Charles was going to call on her, and when she saw him standing in the front room, where Ann had told him to wait for her mistress, she ran into his arms, her joy at seeing him spontaneous and infectious.

'Charles, I cannot believe it is you,' she cried.

He kissed her lips and swung her off her feet, then buried his face in her hair, the old, familiar scent of her body sending waves of delight through him. For want of money, he had lately proposed to La Grande Mademoiselle, but for no other reason. Part of his heart was welded to Lucy's and he accepted that weakness in himself.

'I could not keep away,' he murmured in her ear.

'How is Jamie?' he enquired, looking around for the child.

'He is a proper little Cavalier, now. You would not recognise him, for he has grown into such a little man since you have been away,' said Lucy with pride.

Just then, a dark, angelic looking child appeared and stood shyly by the door.

'Jamie, Papa has come to see you,' said Lucy, as Charles bent to pick the little boy up. If this child had been his legitimate heir, things would be so much simpler, thought Charles, but he had come to learn that life was rarely simple. Mary had heard the noise and she joined them now, all curls and dimples, looking so much like Lucy that Charles felt a rush of tenderness towards her, and wished that she had been his child. Scooping Mary into his arms as well, he covered the two dark heads with kisses.

That night, holding Lucy in his arms, Charles felt at peace for a little while. He had been tired when he arrived, but when darkness fell, he knew that, with Lucy, his tiredness would disappear, as it always had. The first, wild passions he had felt for Lucy when their love was young, had long gone, but he knew his desire for her would always remain. She satisfied deep longings in him, in a way no other woman could. Kingship required that a legitimate heir be produced and marry he would have to, some time, but Lucy would have to be in the background, always.

'Lucy, I have something for you.'

Lucy was drowsy after Charles's lovemaking and turned her heavy eyes towards him, expecting to see some small trifle. He reached over her body and felt in his jacket pocket until the pearls were in his hand. He held them up and in the twilight in the room, they glowed lustrously. Even in her sleepy state, Lucy could see they were beautiful jewels and sat up straight to hold the necklace.

'Charles,' she gasped, 'however were you able to buy these for me?'

'Never mind that. Do you like them?'

'How could I not like them?' said Lucy in wonderment. 'They are so heavy and so perfect.'

She brought her body down on his to kiss him, still holding the heavy necklace in her hand. If he had been able to give her more, he would have, for Lucy would always be the greatest love of his life.

'Lucy, you are the queen of my heart,' he whispered, his voice husky from loving her to the point of exhaustion. A few months ago, and he would have said that it was only Lucy's body that made him come alive, only Lucy's kisses that set fire to his emotions. Just a few months ago and he would have given Lucy a crown, if it had been within his power to do so, but all that had changed now. Lucy had betrayed him with other men, but Charles had enough wisdom to know that the time for recriminations was long gone. All that was left to him were the shards of their love, and they would have to do.

Matters in Cologne needed Charles's attention and he had to leave the next day. He had hopes that Spain would help him regain his throne and, besides, a King did not have time to lie in bed with his mistress all day. Lucy was a little sad to see him go, but only a little, for there was always other company to be had. Before she arranged the night's entertainment, she must show off her beautiful new necklace.

'Ann,' she called, 'Ann, come and see what the King has given me.'

Ann came in, carrying Mary in her arms. Lucy held the necklace up so Ann could admire the lustrous gleam of the beads, the diamond clasp that split the light into all the colours of the rainbow.

'Mary try it,' said Lucy's little daughter, snatching at it.

Lucy dangled it in front of the child.

'You may look at it, Mary, but you must not touch it.'

'You will have to be very careful with that, my lady,' said Ann, 'for it looks to me as if it is worth a King's ransom.'

Lucy laughed delightedly.

'You may be right, Ann. King Charles is very generous to me and he does like to spoil me when he can.'

'He spoils you a great deal more than you deserve,' thought Ann, but said nothing.

It was a few days following Charles's departure when Thomas Howard, Master of the Horse to the Princess of Orange, presented himself at Mistress Lucy Barlow's house in Rotterdam. Lucy was surprised to see him, but the sight of a good-looking man always cheered her spirits.

'I have been sent by the Princess Mary to pay my regards. I trust I do not arrive at a time that inconveniences you?'

'I am delighted to meet you, Sir,' said Lucy.

'How nice of Mary to be so thoughtful as to ask you to call. I am gratified that she still thinks of me.'

Howard explained to Lucy that he was in Rotterdam on official business and would be there for a number of weeks. His visit was brief and when Lucy bade him farewell, she did not expect to see him again, so it was with some surprise that Ann informed her he had called again the next day.

'You may tell him to wait in the back parlour. I will be down in a few minutes.'

Lucy looked in the glass to check her appearance and there was a glint in her eyes as she pulled a comb thoughtfully through her hair. So, Tom Howard was paying his respects again that day and, presumably, it was not because the Princess of Orange, his employer, had asked him to call, but that he wanted to see her again.

'What an unexpected pleasure,' said Lucy, looking at the man who she could not call handsome but found interesting, all the same.

'I will come straight to the point, Mistress Barlow. After seeing you yesterday, I could not stop thinking of you and had to return for one more glance of you.'

He said it lightheartedly and Lucy laughed at the compliment. She understood Tom Howard perfectly. He was married to an older woman, he was in Rotterdam and he wanted company. She should have realised all that yesterday. How stupid she had been. Now that they understood one another, why, there was no need to beat about the bush.

'You have a pretty turn of phrase for a man used to spending his time among horses.'

'You forget I have been connected with the Court for many years and do not spend all my time in the stables.'

'That is so and I was forgetting.'

Very soon, Tom Howard became so frequent a visitor in the house that many of Lucy's other admirers began to think it a waste of time to attempt to contact her. In the few weeks that Tom Howard was in Rotterdam it seemed to Lucy as if he had always been a part of her household. She watched him dandling Mary on his knee and playing kings with Jamie at the same time.

'You must not let your crown slip off your head,' he said to Jamie, who was wearing a cardboard crown that Howard had made him.

There was nothing too much trouble for Tom Howard to do for the children or Lucy, but Ann was suspicious of him.

'We do not really know who he is,' said Ann to the cook one day.

'Oh, yes I know he has been Master of the Horse to Princess Mary, but why is he spending so much time here? I don't like it, but it's no use my saying anything to my lady, for she would not have a word said against him, so fond of him is she.'

In Cologne, Chancellor Hyde was uneasy. Rumours had come to him that Tom Howard was a spy and now he had been told he was taking too much of an interest in Lucy Walter, or Barlow as she was now calling herself.

'Your Majesty must be aware that there are traitors everywhere,' said the loyal Hyde, 'and you mixed with Howard when you stayed with your sister at The Hague. Now, it appears, he is bedding Mistress Barlow. Why?'

Charles's face darkened. How could any man resist Lucy's charms or keep out of her bed?

'I like not this turn of events,' said Hyde. 'There is more to this than meets the eye. I'll swear Howard is in the pay of Cromwell. He need not travel to Rotterdam if he wants a woman — there should be plenty among the Princess of Orange's serving maids who would be willing to satisfy him, I'll warrant. He is with Mistress Barlow to find out all he can about Your Majesty and use it to your harm, mark my words.'

A frown creased Charles's brow momentarily. There were spies everywhere as far as he was concerned and there was little point in getting worked up over this one.

'He knows no more than the man in the street,' said Charles. 'I would not give him a second thought. As for Lucy, she knows nothing that would betray me.'

Hyde sighed. He wished he shared the King's confidence. Charles should be on his guard more, be less trusting of other people. A King could not be too careful.

'If Mistress Barlow left the Continent I would breathe more easily. A pension might help her make up her mind.'

Charles looked sharply at Hyde. Sending Lucy back to England was a drastic measure, but he knew Edward Hyde spoke good sense.

'Where will I get the money to grant Lucy a pension? I am already hard-pressed. I keep body and soul together by a spider's web and a litte help from my sister Mary. However, I will discuss it with Mary and see what she says.'

Hyde nodded agreement. He wished the King would

sever his ties with this woman who was becoming acutely embarrassing.

* * *

Tom Howard had returned to The Hague and Lucy had resumed her usual lifestyle, but Ann sensed her mistress was not well. Her face had a certain pallor that Ann had not seen before and there were dark circles around her eyes.

Some days, she lay on her bed with the curtains drawn and now even Jamie and Mary begging her to get up would not make any difference.

'I have a fair idea of what is wrong with the her again,' said Ann to the cook one day. 'It is the same that was wrong with her not so long ago, I'll warrant. Getting too fond of the castor oil and tansy, lately, and now she has gone and spoilt her health.'

Ann was not sure whose child she had been carrying this time, for there had been many other men after Tom Howard. Lucy probably did not know herself. It annoyed the servant that Lucy had come to this sorry plight. Many women died after doing what she had and if she died, what would become of Jamie and Mary?

'You are not well, my lady, are you?' said Ann, entering Lucy's darkened room. Lucy looked at her with weary eyes. She did not want the servant probing too closely.

'I am not myself.'

'How do you feel?'

'I must have caught a fever, for I am aching.

Beads of sweat were breaking out on Lucy's temple and her voice was weak.

The last time this had happened, Lucy had been strong enough to regain her health quickly, but this time, for whatever reason, she could not.

'Here, let me wipe your face.'

Lucy lay back, apathetically, on the pillows while the servant swabbed the damp flannel over her face and neck.

Her nightgown was saturated in perspiration and Ann went to the linen press and took out a clean one.

'You will have to sit up in bed for me to change you.'

Lucy held her arms obediently above her head while her nightdress was removed. It was then that the servant saw the bottom half of the garment was caked in blood. This was all the confirmation she needed that Lucy had aborted the child she had been carrying. Anger and hatred over Lucy's action and way of life bubbled up inside her. Fury made her say things that normally she would have kept quiet about.

'So, it is as I thought. You have rid yourself of the child.'

If Lucy was surprised at this outburst, she was too ill to show much reaction, but she had the wit not to betray herself.

'What are you talking about? What child do you mean? You are going mad, Ann Hill, mad. Keep your evil thoughts to yourself, else there will be no room for you in this house and you will have to seek employment elsewhere.'

'I'll not go elsewhere. I will stay with you, for I know too much about you and all the goings on here for you to get rid of me. Oh no, you'll not get rid of me with a dose of castor oil and a brew of tansy, like you've done with the other two babes.'

Lucy showed no reaction, which angered Ann even more.

'Change my nightdress, woman, before I catch my death of cold and then you will be charged with my murder.'

Ungraciously, Ann pulled the clean shift over Lucy's head and settled her back on the bed.

'If anyone should be charged with murder, then it is you, my lady,' she said, going out through the door.

'Your tongue has carried away your senses,' replied her mistress, not caring whether she heard or not.

'Blast the woman,' muttered Lucy under her breath.

'She is nothing but a thorn in my side. For two pins I would dismiss her, but Jamie and Mary would miss her.'

'I will get the doctor, that's what I'll do,' said Ann down

in the kitchen, where the cook and the maid were agog to know of Lucy's plight.

'There will be no concealing her wicked ways from him. He will see immediately what she has been up to.'

The next day Doctor Rufus listened gravely while Ann told him of her suspicions about Lucy, but made no comment.

'You will show me to the lady's bedroom, if you please.'

He looked at Lucy wih sympathetic eyes. Whatever she had done, she deserved to be treated in the best possible way he could. The doctor was with her for half an hour and said he would return in a few days time to see how she was. Ann met him at the bottom of the stairs, her eyes full of curiosity, but he said nothing that might betray Lucy's condition.

'Your mistress is not in any kind of danger, but I have left a bottle of physick. You are to see that she takes it every hour. Keep the room ventilated and provide some light nourishment.' And then he was gone.

'Well, what do you make of that?' said Ann to the cook.

'He would never break a confidence,' said the cook.

'I knew he would tell you nothing.'

'Well, we know, without being told, what her ladyship has been up to,' said Ann, sarcastically.

The doctor had not shut the bedroom door and Lucy had heard the conversation that had been going on downstairs. This was too much, that Ann should be gossiping about her. One day, for sure, she would shut that woman's mouth.

Whatever the doctor had put in the medicine seemed to agree with Lucy, for when he came back to visit her, she was up and dressed and greeted him with a smile.

'I trust you are feeling better?' he enquired.

'Yes, there is no need for you to ask,' said Lucy, 'for you can see that I am quite myself again.'

He breathed a sigh of relief. He had faith in his medicine, but it was not infallible.

'I would not venture out of doors just yet, but you can go downstairs, if you wish.'

With a smile he was gone. No, she would not even go downstairs, yet, thought Lucy. She would reserve her strength and tonight she would act.

Lucy had no callers that night and the household was in bed early. Ann slept in the attic. It was not a room that Lucy visited, but she was sure of her way in the dark. She would not use a candle, it might only warn Ann of her arrival. As quietly as she could, she opened the drawer of the chest that contained the bodkin, then, holding the sharp end in the palm of her hand, she crept quietly up the stairs.

She knew Ann was asleep, for she could hear her snoring lightly. If she was lying on her side, then it would make things easier.

Pushing open the door, the shape of the servant was discernible in the moonlight that streamed in through the thin curtain. It seemed that fate was playing into Lucy's hands, for Ann was lying on her side.

All she had to do was find her ear, then thrust the bodkin in as quickly and deeply as she could. Moving aside Ann's sleeping cap, Lucy brought the bodkin into position. It was then that Ann woke up with a scream.

'Oh, Ann, I must have been sleep walking,' said Lucy. 'It must be the medicine Doctor Rufus gave me. He said it was powerful.'

'Sleep walking! Get out of this room and stay out. Don't ever come near me again. Wait!' she said, spotting the instrument in Lucy's hand.

Gripping Lucy tightly by the wrist, she seized the instrument from her.

'So that's it. Not content to murder unborn babes, you thought you would have a try at murdering me as well. Well, let me tell you this, if we were in England, I could have you hanged for this. No good saying you were Charles Stuart's woman then. That would not save you with the Protector.' She gave an ugly laugh. 'You'll not dismiss me, my lady. I shall wait with you as long as it pleases me.'

'You are being silly, Ann. I have a medical condition and

Doctor Rufus would swear that it was the medication that is responsible for my actions. I could never wish you any harm, you know that.'

That was the trouble with Lucy, thought Ann, she would never admit responsibility for her actions. Well, Ann knew to be on her guard now. Lucy would stop at nothing.

* * *

Acting on Hyde's misgivings over Lucy and Howard, Charles visited Mary in The Hague.

'I know your feelings for Lucy have hardened,' began Charles.

'I can only wish yours had too,' replied Mary testily.

'Tom Howard has been seeing her in Rotterdam. His interest in her is unusually keen.'

'Howard was there on my instructions. It was I who sent him, to find out what that little madam is up to.'

'There is no need for bitterness to come into this conversation,' said Charles. It upset him that Mary was venomous towards Lucy now.

'Was it you who told him to spend his nights in Lucy's bed? Was that part of his duties, too?'

Charles had caught Mary off her guard now, and her head jerked up in surprise.

'Yes, spies come to me, also, and tell me things, and Howard is not a man I would like to trust too closely.'

'How can you say that. You hardly know the man. He has been my servant for years and I have found no fault with him, no fault at all.'

'Ah, Mary, you must guard against trusting people too much,' said her brother.

'What if I were to tell you that Tom Howard is in the pay of Cromwell?'

'You do not know that,' flashed his sister, 'That is merely surmise on your part.'

'Well, if it is a guess, then it is a good guess, and you would do well to be wary of the man.'

Charles drew in his breath. He disliked arguing, especially with Mary who had been so good to him. He dropped the tone of his voice.

'Mary, I only want to protect you and myself. We cannot be sure who our friends are in times like this.'

He took her hands in his. Mary was widowed now and had a small son of her own. Her position in the Netherlands was not as strong as it had been when her husband was alive, but he knew she would always help him, if she could.

'I have come to speak to you about Lucy. Chancellor Hyde wants her back in England; he thinks the further away from me she is, the safer I will be.'

Glancing at Mary, Charles could see that what he had said struck a chord with his sister.

'The question is, how do we get her to go to England voluntarily?'

Charles could see from Mary's eyes, her thoughts were moving rapidly.

'If she were to be granted a pension, we might be able to persuade her to leave the Continent.'

Mary understood now why Charles had come to her to discuss Lucy.

'And what you require from me, is the money for the pension?'

'I hate to have to ask you, Mary, but I have no means of my own, save what you give me and occasional money from sympathisers in England. A peripatetic court does not come cheap, and I am always casting around for new ways to live frugally.'

Mary understood that what Charles had said was true. The monarchy was bankrupt and not only Charles, but Henrietta Maria and Minette lived on the charity of their French cousins.

'She shall have the money, Charles, for your sake,' said Mary, quietly. The King embraced his sister.

'Mary, when I am restored, your kindness will not be forgotten.'

Charles spent no more than a few days with Mary, but they were long enough for Daniel O'Neil to make himself indispensable as Groom of the Bedchamber to Charles.

'Why don't you take him back to Cologne with you?' said Mary.

'I do not need him at the moment, so he can stay with you for as long as you have employment for him.'

Mary was so generous that Charles did not want to accept more than was necessary from her, but she was insistent now.

'You have him, for since William's death, I do not always have a ready occupation for him. I should tell you that he is married to Tom Howard's mother-in-law.'

Daniel O'Neil took a pride in his new job and soon made himself indispensable to the King. He was quiet and courteous in his manner but he had a quick intelligence and a ready grasp of what was happening around him.

Charles wasted no time in telling Hyde that he could speak to Lucy regarding the pension.

'I have spoken with my sister and she has agreed that the lady be paid a pension.'

A look of satisfaction spread across Hyde's face. The King would know no peace until that woman was out of the way. He knew Charles had enjoyed many dalliances and been indiscreet, but no other woman remained to make him look foolish, like Lucy did.

'As soon as I have your command, I will be on my way to inform Mistress Barlow — more than she deserves, I would say.'

Charles laughed. Hyde could not resist his two pennorth where Lucy was concerned.

'On your way, then, before my sister changes her mind.'

* * *

Lucy had not seen her brother Justus since she had been on the Continent, but when he wrote to tell her he would be visiting her, she was pleased.

'The guest bedroom will be prepared for Mr. Walter,' she instructed Ann.

'He will be arriving within the next few days.'

How good it would be to see Justus again. They had always understood each other so well. In his letter, Justus told Lucy that he was taking time off from his work at the Bar for he had been working too hard for a long while.

Lucy greeted Justus with genuine delight, hugging and kissing him and holding Jamie and Mary up so they could be kissed as well.

'Lucy, my little sister, who is now a mother,' laughed Justo.

'And I am an uncle and have not forgotten my duties as such,' he said, giving Jamie a whip and top and Mary a wooden doll. The children squealed with delight at these unexpected treats, and settled down to play with their toys.

'Come, Lucy, while they are able to amuse themselves, I have details to discuss with you. Our mother's will has been proved and there is a sum of money to come to each of us. Your share amounts to over a thousand pounds and we must go to London to claim our portions some time.'

Lucy's face brightened up at the thought of the money, for when Elizabeth Walter had died, Lucy little thought she would have had anything to leave.

Lucy was in a flurry, though she did not show it. Every day, it seemed, something new and exciting was happening to her. Now it was the Kings's old Chancellor, Edward Hyde, who had been to make her an offer of a pension as long as she left the Netherlands and never set foot on the shores again!

'Justo, Justo, come quickly!' she called, when Ann had shown Hyde out.

'Whatever next!' she said excitedly to her startled brother. 'I have been offered a pension!'

She pirhouetted around the room, then as Mary came in through the door, caught her up in her arms and danced with her.

'Mamma's been offered a pension, Mary,' she said to the uncomprehending child.

'Lucy, sit down and calm down,' said her brother. Justus knew that Lucy showed this excitable side of her personality only to her family; to others she could appear outwardly calm, whatever the occasion.

'Who was that man who just left?' demanded her brother, thinking he might have been a grateful admirer of Lucy's.

'Is he one of your older gentlemen?'

Lucy dissolved into peals of laughter.

'Oh, Justo, you are hopeless. An old admirer!' and she laughed again.

'That,' she said, emphasising the word, 'that was no less than Chancellor Edward Hyde, sent by His Majesty to offer Mistress Lucy Barlow a pension,' and she twirled around the floor again.

'Lucy, Lucy, come and sit down and explain it to me — but first call Ann to take Mary to the garden to play with Jamie so we can have some peace.'

When Lucy had told Justo everything Hyde had said, he sat contemplatively for a while, watching the sunlight glancing off the brass candlesticks and illuminating specks of dust floating in the air. At last he spoke.

'It's a good offer Lucy. The best you are likely to have at the moment. You, and the children, would be secure for life. After all, what have you got here? Not much, aye?'

Lucy did not like the last remarks her brother had made, true though they were.

'I have been happy here,' she said, in an attempt to justify her position.

'Oh, come now, Lucy, you could be just as happy in London and have a pension to fall back on. I do not think you have any choice other than to accept the offer gracefully.'

'Why should I allow myself to be pushed around by the King and his ministers? What if it does not suit me to move? Why should I be told what to do?'

'Lucy, I do not mean to be ungallant, for to me you will always be my beautiful little sister, but you are not growing any younger. What will become of you when you are old? The King has offered you the money, take it before the offer is withdrawn.'

Lucy's eyes grew serious. There was sense in what her brother said.

Charles gave her enough money to live on in Rotterdam and her nightly visitors gave her enough gilders to make life pleasant, but if she had the pension, she would be better off in England than she was in Rotterdam. Then and there, she made her mind up — she would accept the pension and leave quietly.

'I have made my mind up.'

Justus watched her intently.

'I shall accept the pension.'

Her brother smiled in relief.

'Good. We shall write the letter immediately and get it off to Cologne as soon as possible. You have made a wise move. And, remember, if King Charles is restored to his throne, the Cavaliers will return to England!'

Lucy looked at her brother. He did not condemn her. Although his nature was entirely different from hers, he knew, that for Lucy, to live was to love. Anything less would be nothing short of death.

With Justus to help her, Lucy made preparations to return to England. 'Oh, Lordy!' cried Ann, 'to think that we are to return to England at last. Oh! I can't believe it.' And she ran to tell the cook and the maid that soon they would vacate the little house in the back streets of Rotterdam.

Like an albatross that hovers over a sinking ship, Tom Howard returned to haunt Lucy with his presence in the days before her return to England. Lucy was delighted to see him.

'I happened to find myself in Rotterdam and had to call to see you,' and he smiled at Lucy in that lazy way of his, sensuous lips revealing good, even teeth. Yes, he had been pleased when Cromwell had given him his orders to return to Rotterdam, making it look as though he were there by command of the Princess Mary, then offering to escort Mistress Barlow and her party to London. He saw no reason why business could not be mixed with pleasure. Why, the lady liked it as much as himself, so who was grumbling?

Lucy introduced Justus to Tom Howard and the two young men appeared to get on well. It was the morning before they were ready to leave that Justus and Lucy were sitting drinking chocolate and discussing Howard, that a thought struck Justus.

'Lucy, did you know that Tom Howard knew our grandfather Protheroe?'

'No,' said Lucy. 'How do you know he knew him?'

'We were talking about this and that and I mentioned that when we left Pembrokeshire we lived in Kinge Street, Covent Garden, and then Howard said he had lived there, too, and he knew Grandfather.'

'Well, what's wrong with that?'

Her brother shook his head slowly.

'I did not say there was anything wrong with that, it just seems strange that he did not mention it to you sooner.'

Seeing he was going to get no response from his sister, he said,

'Oh, well, it takes all sorts but, Lucy, perhaps we should be on our guard. It's funny how he should turn up again now.'

For answer, his sister looked determinedly out of the window.

That evening, Tom Howard arrived and announced to Lucy and Justo that he had booked a passage on the same boat as them.

'It was a spur of the moment decision. When I heard you were going to London, it made me homesick to see the old place again, so I am coming with you.'

Justus said nothing. It seemed too much of a coincidence to him.

When he had gone, Justus tackled Lucy.

'Does that chap Howard know anything about your pension, Lucy?'

'Not a thing. At least, I have not said anything to anyone other than you about it. Why do you ask?'

'That man's after something. I'll wager. I'm not as keen on him as you are, and the more I see of him, the less I like him.'

'Oh Justo, please don't be difficult now. Soon we will be in London and that will be the end of Tom.'

Her brother felt uneasy about the man, despite what Lucy said.

'Justus, I have something to show you,' said Lucy.

Going to a drawer, she unlocked it and brought out a suede wallet.

'Look what I have here' and she took out the pearl necklace that Charles had given her.

'Where did you get that?'

Lucy explained the King had given it to her.

I'm no expert, but even I can see that it is a valuable gift.'

'It was given to me as security, so if I was ever in need, I would have something to sell.'

Lucy's eyes were sparkling.

'I cannot wait to get to London. It will all be so exciting. The first thing I am going to do is to order a coach. It will be one of the best coaches in London. I shall have it lined in red velvet, fringed in gold and the outside shall be gilded, so that it glistens in the sun. We will look, for all the world, like royalty. How would you like to travel in a coach like that?'

'Lucy, do not spend all your money at once,' pleaded her brother, 'and do not attract too much attention to yourself. A great display of spending does not do at times like this. The London we are going to is not the London you knew. Times have changed and the gaiety has gone. It is not wise to look as though you might be a friend of the King's. There are Puritan soldiers on every street corner, spying, and it is best to dress drably'.

'Fie, Justus. You are talking like an old woman and making me feel quite out of sorts. I can do without talk like that. Come, I'll have no more of your dreary misgivings. We are going to London and we are going to enjoy ourselves!'

As they waited on the quayside in Flushing the next morning to board the boat for England, Justus looked at Lucy, remembering the conversation they had had the previous day. If it were possible to enjoy life in Cromwell's England, then he was sure Lucy would. His eyes, like Lucy's, were following a skein of wild geese, winging through the cold dawn. The birds, like them, were seeking new adventures, but unlike himself, they were free from misgivings.

If Justus Walter had known what fate was to await them in England, none of the party would ever have set foot on the boat that morning.

A small coaling vessel pulled alongside the jetty, and the sailors, with faces as tanned as their leathern breeches, jumped ashore to help the party with their luggage.

'Careful with that bag,' called Lucy to one of the younger ones who was about to throw the bag with the pearl necklace into the hold.

He turned and stared insolently, then took a deep pull on his pipe and blew a mouthful of smoke into her face.

'Insolent fellow,' said Justus.

With that, the captain appeared and rebuked the man, apologising to Lucy on his behalf. As the fellow turned away, he was heard to say,

'So what? A cat may look at a queen.'

Chapter 8

Apartments had been rented for Lucy above a barber's shop, near to Somerset House. Justus was to stay with Lucy while their mother's will was being administered.

'Would there be any objections if I stayed as well?' enquired Tom Howard. Justus gave him a guarded look.

'I would rent my own rooms, naturally, for I would not wish you to be cramped.'

'We will all be pleased if you stay, Colonel Howard, won't we, Justus?'

'You must do as you wish, Lucy, for I must return to my work before long.' Jamie and Mary were pleased 'Uncle Tom' was staying, for he could always think of new games to play.

'Uncle Tom will play Kings and Queens with Jamie and Mary,' lisped Mary, happily.

Justus had warned Lucy that the London she had known had disappeared, but nothing he said had prepared her for the depressing sight of the dismal poverty she saw, the fatigued poor in the back streets, eking out their meagre days, diseased and beaten. Yet the Port of London was brimming with shipping from foreign lands, bringing corn, oil, spices and wine to gladden the hearts of the rich. Was it the sight of lavish wealth, contrasting so violently with festering poverty, that upset her? She could not be sure, but as she was unable to help the poor, she meant to enjoy herself.

Lucy had a triumphant look in her eyes soon after their arrival in London.

'I promised you we would have a coach, Justus, and it will be ready for us very soon. We will ride all over London. Jamie and Mary can feed the ducks in Saint James's Park and I would like to ride down Lincoln's Inn Fields and see the lovely houses.'

Her brother nodded. Lucy was irrepressible. When they were young, it was always Lucy who could think of new adventures for them, Lucy who could wheedle Marie into taking the pony and trap to Newgale sands with Lucy and Justus aboard, but now it was he who knew more about London than his sister.

'The Pleasure Gardens have been closed by order of the killjoys, but there are means of enjoying oneself, if you know where to go,' he said, slowly.

'Oh, Justus, tell me what we can do at night.'

'We might go and watch a performance at Drury Lane of one of Sir William Davenant's plays and, later, we could have boeuf à la mode in the 'The Bluebells' in Covent Garden.'

Lucy clapped her hands in delight. She had some money and she was going to enjoy herself in London. She had set her mind to it.

'You and I will go out one night, very soon.'

Her brother nodded. Howard had disappeared soon after their arrival, saying he had old acquaintances to look up. Justus was relieved that he was not there, but he could not help wondering what he was up to. Lucy could see her brother was in a thoughtful mood.

'Why have you been so quiet since our arrival?' she queried. 'I thought you were looking forward to having me back, but, often, all I get from you is long silences or blank stares.'

'Of course I am pleased you are in London again, Lucy, but I do not trust that man Howard and instinct tells me he is up to no good.'

'Rubbish. How can you say that? His credentials are impeccable. Princess Mary would not have him as Master of the Horse if she had any doubt about him. You are being silly. What could he be up to? He is our friend, he chose to travel over with us and has even taken an apartment in the same house as us. Whatever you may think, I see no harm in him. Have I convinced you now?'

Her brother nodded, to please Lucy, but he felt unhappy about the situation. It was not something he could explain rationally, but it was an uneasy feeling, always hovering somewhere at the back of his mind.

*   *   *

'I think that was a most successful evening,' remarked Lucy as she and Justus lingered over a glass of wine. It was a few days since Justus had raised his anxieties over Tom Howard, but he appeared to have put his misgivings out of the way for the time being, at least, and they had spent a pleasant evening in the company of legal friends of Justus. Justus noticed how well Lucy looked when in the company of the opposite sex. Many admiring glances were thrown her way and Lucy had sparkled. Flattery and charm never went amiss; they were like life-blood to her. Justus had been aware for a long time that she was a woman who could never be happy without a man. He prodded the last few sparks out of the smouldering logs with the toe of his boot and turned his mind to his comfortable bed, when heavy footsteps were heard outside. Brother and sister looked at each other enquiringly. Before either could speak, loud, demanding knocking came from the front door.

'Open up in the name of the law.'

Lucy threw Justus a terrified look.

'I'll go. You wait here and don't move.'

Lucy's thoughts flew to Jamie and Mary. She hoped they had heard nothing. As the heavy door was unbolted, there was a babble of noise, a commotion and above it all, Justus's voice.

'On what authority do you come here?'

'We are here by command of the Lord Protector to arrest

Mistress Lucy Barlow, her maidservant Ann Hill, her brother Justus Walter and her two children and take them directly to the Tower of London.'

Lucy's throat constricted. Could she have understood correctly what she had heard?

'Before you can arrest anyone, you must have a warrant.'

Lucy felt so thankful for Justus's presence. He would help them and know what to do.

'We have a warrant, Sir. Now, lead us to Mistress Barlow.'

Lucy's heart sank.

'There is no need for you all to come in, one will be enough.'

'And who, may I ask, are you, Sir?' asked the Officer in Charge.

'I am Justus Walter and, I should warn you, a member of the Middle Temple and, as such, will appoint legal representatives to act on behalf of my sister and myself. Let me see your warrant.'

A moment's pause and Lucy heard Justus say,

'It seems to be in order. What, exactly, is the charge?'

'Spying for King Charles II, Sir, that is the charge.'

'You had better come this way.'

Justus took the soldier into the room where only a few minutes earlier the atmosphere had been happy and convivial. He would have done anything to spare Lucy from this ordeal, but, since the Colonel's papers were in order, there was little more he could do this night for Lucy, or for any of them.

One of Lucy's strengths was that in difficult circumstances, she kept her composure. Standing up, she faced the officer.

'I have heard everything that has transpired between you and my brother. We have no choice other than to accompany you, but your master shall answer for this. It is a shame and a disgrace to call on law abiding citizens at this hour, disturbing the night's peace.'

At this, the Puritan looked a little shamefaced.

'Do you know my children are sleeping?'

Lucy's words were bravely spoken, but her eyes filled with tears at the mention of Jamie and Mary.

'Do not upset yourself now, Lucy,' whispered Justus. 'I will see that we have the best legal advice available.'

Lucy felt some comfort flow from Justus to herself.

'I will go and wake Jamie and Mary. Ann will have to help me dress them.'

Ann was awake and standing on the landing when Lucy went upstairs. She had not missed any of the proceedings. It was the servant who spoke first, unable to contain her anger a moment longer.

'It is you who have done this to me. Your spite knows no bounds, does it, my lady?'

'Ann, do not be ridiculous. I have done nothing to you. We are all being arrested, even Justus, Jamie and Mary. Would to God that I had the power to save us all from this, but I cannot. Tomorrow, Justus will engage a lawyer. I do not want to go to the Tower any more than you do, but there is nothing we can do about it tonight. Get dressed, then come and help me with Jamie and Mary. We must try to see that they are not too upset.'

As Lucy was packing, Justus managed to whisper to her, despite the watchful eyes of the Colonel, to take her pension warrant with her.

'Admit to nothing until we have seen a lawyer.'

At last, two sleepy children were taken outside to the waiting carriage.

Lucy found some sweetmeats to soothe them and Jamie held his coral rattle with the silver bells. He always dropped off to sleep with it in his hand and Lucy made sure he did not forget it. The leather curtains of the coach were drawn and Lucy settled herself as best she could on the uncomfortable seats. She could not help thinking the coach that had been provided for them lacked the comfort of the carriage they were used to. There were no stars in the sky, that dark night, but even if there had been, Lucy would have been in no mood to appreciate them. Her thoughts were on Tom Howard, conspicuous by his absence.

'Where is Tom Howard tonight?' asked Justus, grimly, echoing her thoughts. 'He is at the root of this. I can see it all now!' Justus did not want to say any more then, lest Ann Hill heard too much, but it was all beginning to add up in his mind. Charles had given Lucy a pension to put her out of the way. Merely sending Lucy to London was not good enough for Mary, Princess of Orange, though. She had plotted to put Lucy away for a long time, in the Tower of London, which she might never leave alive. No wonder the Princess of Orange had been generous in granting Colonel Howard extended leave.

At the Tower, Lucy and her children were shown into a cold, comfortless room. Lucy looked around her in despair. What she did not know was that their room was far superior to that of ordinary prisoners. Oliver Cromwell, though the sworn enemy of kingship, still retained some awe for the mystery that surrounded it. For all he knew, Lucy might be Charles's lawful wife and, as such, he would not treat her like a commoner.

Mary began to cry as Lucy attempted to settle the children down to what remained of the night.

'Do not cry, darling, everything will be better in the morning.' Lucy only wished she felt as confident as she sounded.

Lucy woke to a cheerless dawn, having slept for no more than an hour or so. She felt exhausted. As she splashed her face with cold water, all her worries were for her children. They were not used to being confined in one small room all day. Jamie was high spirited and liked noisy games. He, more than Mary, who was quiet and liked to nurse her doll while listening to a story, would be the one who would suffer the most. Light footsteps were heard in the corridor outside and they hesitated by Lucy's door. She heard whispering outside, then the door opened and two women warders stood there, spite arranged over every feature in their faces.

'Oh, look, Martha, this be the lady.'

The other woman's eyes, narrow as the barred slits in the window, murky as the colour of the Thames, bore viciously into Lucy's face.

'Ain't had a lady here for a long time, have we, Martha, but we knows a lady when we sees one and we knows how to treat a lady when we meets one, don't we?'

With that, the woman who had been speaking crossed the room to where Lucy was standing, lifted her skirt and petticoats in the air, giving a whoop as she did so. Lucy stood still, too shocked to move as her petticoats floated back around her. Then the woman spat in Lucy's face and the two of them began laughing, a hollow, rattling sound, mirthless as the iron clank of Tyburn's knockers. They had not finished yet, for they meant to have their sport, and more.

'Don't she looked shocked, May?'

'She do, but she'll just have to get used to our little ways, for we do like our fun, don't we?' and she tweaked Lucy's cheek hard, till it stung. 'My lady's going to be here for a long' and to add emphasis, she rolled her eyes, 'long time.'

Jamie and Mary had woken up and huddled together on the bed, their faces white, eyes as wide as hunted does.

'What do ladies have, Martha?'

'Jewels, May.'

Dropping the bantering tone, the one called May grabbed Lucy by the arm and dug her broken nails into Lucy's white flesh. 'We'll have your jewels now, my girl.' She resumed her former tone, 'We like pretty things, don't we, May?' then she released Lucy, pushing her roughly backwards, till her head banged against the wall and a searing pain shot down her neck. Seeing Lucy's pain, the woman laughed again. Jamie and Mary began to cry.

'Those two brats can shut their traps, else we'll do it for them.

There'll be plenty of work for the young master and little lady to keep them quiet later on.'

Lucy put her arms around the children, begging them not to cry.

'Martha, the carry-all. Open it.'

And before Lucy's petrified eyes, they rummaged through her bag. Lucy was glad she had hidden her jewellery on her person. She was only sorry that she had not taken the precaution of hiding the pension warrant in her bodice. The women were tipping the bag upside down, grunting in their disappointment.

'She's got jewels alright, Martha. If they ain't in the bag, then they be on her.'

Lucy's heart gave a sickening lurch. The necklace Charles gave her was her bulwark against need. If these women found it, Lucy would lose it for ever.

'We'll soon find out where she's keeping her bits and pieces. We'll strip her.' She moved menacingly towards Lucy. At least they had not noticed the pension warrant and Lucy was thankful for that.

The other woman, who was still rummaging through the tipped contents was holding a piece of paper up to the light, casting her eyes uncomprehendingly over it.

'There's some paper here, Martha,' she said, slowly.

'Throw it away,' the other commanded.

Lucy's head was throbbing, her vision misty and a feeling of unreality was sweeping over her, but she heard her voice call out, as though it belonged to someone else.

'Give that paper to me.'

Before the women could respond a man's shape loomed in the doorway and the two women sprang to their feet.

'Get out of here now, this minute and I do not want to see either of you near Mistress Barlow again.'

The woman who had been holding the warrant dropped it and the man bent down and handed the paper to Lucy, but not before he had seen the signature.

'Yours, I believe, Madam.'

It was Sir John Barkstead, Lieutenant of the Tower, who had come to Lucy's rescue. He looked at Lucy with sympathetic eyes.

'You will not be troubled by those two again,' he said, watching their departing figures.

'Mistress Walter, or perhaps I should say Barlow?'

'I am known as Barlow, Sir,' replied Lucy quietly.

'Well then, Mistress Barlow, perhaps you would like to tell me something of the nature of your visit to this country?'

'My mother has lately died, and I have been left a sum of money, more than one thousand pounds. I came over so that I might receive what my mother intended me to have.'

'Now I must ask you questions of a personal nature. I believe you have two children. Am I right?'

'I have a boy and a girl, Sir, and they are with me here in the Tower.'

'Rumour has it that the King is the boy's father. Is he the father of the girl as well?'

These were the questions Lucy had been expecting and she had slept very little the previous night, going over in her mind how she would answer the questions. At all costs, she must not let it be thought that Jamie was Charles's child, else he might never be released from the Tower.

'I had a son by Charles Stuart, Sir, but he is now dead. The children I have with me are by a husband I had in Holland.'

'Where is this husband now?' asked the Lieutenant. His manner did not seem entirely unsympathetic and Lucy did not find it difficult talking to him.

'My husband, alas, is dead.'

Sir John nodded his head.

'When did you last see King Charles?'

Lucy paused a moment, not that she could not remember when she last saw Charles, but because she wished to appear as though she were trying hard to recall the date.

'I have not seen the King these last two years, Sir,' she replied, eventually.

'Now I believe Colonel Howard was with you in the Netherlands, that he came to London with you and, in fact, lives with you in London. Am I correct?'

Lucy was thankful that she had thought through her story very carefully in advance, for now she was able to answer confidently.

'I met Colonel Howard in Flushing, as I was boarding the ship. Since my arrival in London, I have seen very little of him.'

The Lieutenant scratched his beard for a moment. Mistress Barlow was an impressive witness, sure of her facts. He felt inclined to believe her. It was only Tom Howard's word they had against hers, and he was not the most reliable of witnesses.

'One last question. Have you received your inheritance?'

'I have not received one penny, but hope to be informed to my advantage before long.'

'That will be all Mistress Barlow. I thank you for your information.'

'Sir, before you go, I would like you to see this,' said Lucy, giving the warrant to Sir John. The little he had seen of the document earlier had been enough to convince him it was an official paper. Lucy guessed, shrewdly, that to conceal it would only have added to the question marks already hanging over her.

'If I read it correctly, King Charles II has granted you a pension?'

'That is correct.'

Back in his office, Sir John shook his head ruefully. It was difficult to know what to make of the situation. The lady needed to be treated correctly. For all he knew, she might be the wife of Charles II who had just blown a cloud of smoke in his eyes to hide her true position.

When Sir John had gone, Lucy felt pleased with her performance. Jamie and Charles had not been betrayed, but she had been given no clue as to who had reported her for spying. Someone was eager to see her downfall, but who? She sat down by a window and far below, on the street, a crowd of people had gathered to watch something. After a while, it became clear that they were watching a bear being baited. She sighed. Some things never changed. What had the bear done to harm any of them? She looked at Jamie and Mary, sleeping exhaustedly like innocent babes on the bed. Jamie was clutching his coral rattle, given him at his christening to ward off evil spirits. He needed it now more than ever, if they were to leave the Tower before any more harm came to them. The one thing Lucy feared was Ann Hill's testimony. It could damn them all. Lucy had a feeling that if Ann could save her own skin, she would. If it meant blacking Lucy, she would, with pleasure.

Ann Hill was questioned on the second day of July. She was more than pleased to say what she knew about Lucy Barlow. Yes, Colonel Howard, Gentleman of the Horse to the Princess Royal, often kept Mistress Barlow company. No, she did not know that the lady had a husband in Holland, or anywhere else. Yes, King Charles was the father of the two children. No, it was not two years since the lady saw King Charles. It was the night before they sailed for England. The lady had been given a valuable pearl necklace by the King and she had heard her discuss its value with her brother, Justus Walter. The lady always had clothes aplenty, a rich diet and a coach to attend her from week to week. The lady made her keep to her room at night, so she did not see what was going on and she scarce had the liberty to go downstairs for a cup of ale. The lady had told her, strictly, to say, if asked, that the lady had been the wife of a Dutch captain, now dead. This story she had said to everyone.

The next day, Ann Hill was called in front of the Lieutenant again and her statement was read back to her.

'Do you agree you said what I have just read to you? asked Sir John.

'Yes, Sir,' said Ann.

'Then put your mark on the bottom of the paper, just there,' and he indicated with his finger the place where her name had been printed. The Lieutenant could see by the look of satisfaction on the maid's face that she bore her mistress a grudge. It was often the way with servants, he thought, philosophically. A maid's testimony was nothing to go by. For his part, he was inclined to believe Mistress Barlow innocent of the charge of spying and he would tell the Lord Protector so.

Time did not pass any faster, merely because it did not suit Lucy Barlow to be a prisoner in the Tower. Every hour hung like a leaden weight upon her heart, dragging her spirits lower each minute that passed. She had been a prisoner for only a matter of days, but they seemed like years, when she was summoned to speak to Sir John.

As Lucy entered the room she saw Sir John was not alone. She recognised the other man as being the Lord Protector, Oliver Cromwell. The Lieutenant showed Lucy to a chair and, when she was seated, the Protector spoke.

'I am sorry that we have troubled you and given you this inconvenience, Madam. We acted in good faith on information we had received, believing you to be a spy, working for King Charles II.'

He watched Lucy's face carefully, but it was expressionless. A comelier face he had not seen for many a day and a pretty face was not wasted on Oliver Cromwell. If there was ever an opportunity to please a beautiful woman, then he would. He remembered Frances, Lady Carbery of Dynefor, how she had welcomed him so hospitably, how charmed he had been by her graciousness.

'We have come to the conclusion that we were misinformed.'

Hearing this, Lucy gave a little gasp of relief, parting her lips so prettily that Cromwell gave a little smile. He looked into her expressive eyes and her glance warmed him like a glass of fine Cognac slipping down his throat, making him glad he was in a position to release her.

'We ask one thing of you.'

Lucy was ready to agree to anything as long as they could leave their sombre surroundings as quickly as possible. She hoped she would not see the inside of the Tower ever again. Lucy's eyes met the Protector's and his heart melted.

'You must return to the Continent, whence you came.'

Lucy nodded her head. After this turn of events, London had lost its attractions for her and she would feel safer back in The Hague.

'We will return immediately we are released and can secure passes and passages.'

The Lord Protector looked at the Lieutenant and cleared his throat.

'There will be no need for you to board a cargo vessel. It has been decided you have been inconvenienced enough as it is. A private boat has been arranged for you and you will be set ashore in Flanders.' Although she had been sorely tried over recent events, Lucy's good manners did not desert her. Rising, she replied, 'I give my thanks to you both, good Sirs.'

Oliver Cromwell smiled indulgently. If the King had married Mistress Barlow, he would not have been in the least surprised. There was something about her meek manner that made men want to protect her and she had the voluptuous looks that turned men's heads. He found the Welsh lilt to her voice delightful, for he was of Welsh stock himself. Watching Lucy as she made her way from the room, the sun burnishing her dark ringlets till they sparked a Titian gold, bouncing off her rounded cheeks and glistening on her full lips, he could not help but think there were women whom he had to remind himself were of the female sex and then there were women like Lucy whose laugh, gestures, every movement, signalled she was drenched in delectable, feminine charm. Lucy heard Cromwell say to the Lieutenant as she was leaving, 'Mistress Barlow and her household will be free to leave tomorrow. The Proctor's warrant is being prepared this very moment.'

Back in her room, Lucy was elated.

'Tomorrow we will leave the Tower, Jamie, and you and Mary will soon be able to play outside again.'

Jamie put the coral rattle in his mouth for comfort. It had hardly been out of his hand since they had been there. During their incarceration, Lucy fancied it had grown paler. She wondered if it was her imagination playing tricks on her, or was it true what old wives said that when the child who owned the rattle was unhappy, it lost its colour?

The relief of their impending release was enormous, but Lucy dared not think too much about it, lest there were hitches. That night, she slept very badly. Charles came to her in her dreams, saying he would have no more to do with her. He was sending her back to England, back to the Tower, which she would never leave. At last, morning broke and sanity returned. Charles would never harm her, he would always love her. A part of his heart would belong to her, not to anyone else, throughout their lives and into the eternity that lay beyond.

It had to be Tom Howard who was to blame for all their troubles. Mary was behind this, Mary of Orange, whose friendship had turned sour. Lucy would be very careful of Mary in future. Wearily, she rubbed her eyes. She was tired, Jamie and Mary were upset, Justus had suffered unnecessarily and all because of that cythraul, that devil, Tom Howard. If he had not been so frequently in her bed, she might not have been so annoyed with him. Lucy clenched her fists and bit her lips. Diawl! She'd get even with that scoundrel.

On July, 17, 1656, the Mercurius Politicus reported, most respectfully, that Mistress Barlow and the young heir were set on the shores of Flanders, travelling in a specially commissioned boat. This was no ordinary courtesy.

Once on foreign soil, the lady openly declared her son was the child of Charles II.

'So, that woman is back on the Continent, despite our best efforts,' said Daniel O'Neil, Groom of the King's Bedchamber, addressing the Princess of Orange.

O'Neil had been sent by Charles to tell his sister, Mary, of the latest developments concerning Lucy. O'Neil had as much love for Lucy as did the Princess and he was eager to discuss with her the latest intelligence he had received from Tom Howard, to whose mother-in-law he was married.

'From all accounts the Lord Protector was enchanted with her.'

The Princess's stare was steely.

'We still have our trump card,' she replied, incisively.

O'Neil stared out of the window for a few moments without speaking, then turning to look at Mary, he said, 'You mean Jamie?'

Mary's smile made her features ugly.

'You and I understand each other very well, Colonel. If we remove the child, we destroy Mistress Barlow's power. It is as simple as that.'

'The idea may be simple, but the execution of the deed will be far from easy.'

'Why? What will be difficult about taking a child from a woman? She has no one to defend her — she does not live in a fortress surrounded by guards, does she?'

'I was thinking of the King, Your Highness.'

'What about him?'

'He would prefer it done with Mistress Barlow's agreement, I think, and for the sake of the boy, he would not wish unpleasant scenes.'

'I am not concerned with Lucy's feelings, when she has scant regard for those of others. You will convey my thoughts to the King and he will know what to do.'

Before returning to Bruges, Colonel O'Neil displayed a sound understanding of the rules of espionage. The first thing to do was to keep a close watch on his intended victim, make a note of the time she rose in the morning, who visited her regularly, what time she went out, the hour she retired for the night. To do this, he took rooms in a house opposite Lucy's and he ensured that his view was uninterrupted.

O'Neil had not been stalking his prey for long, when the opportunity presented itself for talking to her maid, whom he espied going marketing. Having seen Ann Hill leave the house with her basket, O'Neil hastened after her. Knowing flattery went a long way with her type, he gave a low bow, a flourish of his hat and began, 'Do I have the honour of addressing Mistress Barlow's maid?'

'Yes, Sir,' said Ann in a fluster. No man had ever given her a second glance before and she was overcome that a gentleman should approach her in the street.

'I would like to talk to you about your mistress.' He could see from the maid's eager expression that she was only too willing to discuss her mistress. The more garrulous she was, the better it would serve his purpose. Catching her by the arm, he said, 'We cannot speak in the street. I would deem it an honour if you were to take a cup of ale with me.'

Guiding her into the back room of one of the inns nearby, O'Neil settled them at a table in a dark corner. Ann's heart was in a flurry.

A gentleman had never treated her in this way before; it gave her a feeling of importance, which led to a willingness to talk. She leaned forward eagerly, saying, 'I will tell you all I know about my mistress, but I cannot be long, for she is expecting me back shortly.'

'My mistress miscarried two children at least, by physick.'

She paused for effect and a triumphant look spread over her face when she saw the look of keen interest on the Colonel's face.

'How do you know this? Did you assist her?'

'Only that I was told to brew the tansy broth for her and after that she was taken very bad.'

'Did a doctor attend her?'

'Only after I called him. Doctor Rufus will not tell you anything, but you ask the cook.'

O'Neil could tell from the animated expression on Ann's face that there were more revelations to come. Leaning forward, so that he would not miss any of the details, she said, 'She tried to kill me.'

'Kill you? Mistress Barlow tried to kill you?' said the incredulous O'Neil.

'Tried to stick a bodkin in my ear, she did,' and the maid nodded, to give emphasis to what she had just said.

'I have not finished with her over that, yet. For two ticks, I would report her to the Seigneur.'

'The Seigneur de Hemfleet?'

'The Seigneur de Hemfleet, Sir, would have her drummed out of the town and country for the scandalous person that she is, if he knew what I know.' O'Neil pulled on his pipe. He did not care what happened to Lucy, only as far as it affected the King. It would be harmful to the image of kingship if the mother of His Majesty's child and the young boy in her care, were made a public exhibition of. Charles's enemies would seize the opportunity to make a laughing stock of him. Monarchy was a fragile concept which could not afford too many detractors. He put his hand inside his jacket to remove his wallet. Ann's glistening eyes watched his movement, like a cat who crouches motionlessly, watching a mouse.

'You have been very helpful to me this morning, madam, and I can see you are a good servant. What would you say to a hundred gilders for keeping your story to yourself? No repeating it to anyone else. Let it be a secret between you and me. You know my meaning?'

Swiftly, Ann's hand reached out to accept the money. She knew what he meant and she knew what a hundred gilders meant; it was a cushion between her and want.

'I'll never breathe another word about it Sir, not as long as I live, I never will.'

Despite the servant's assurance, O'Neil decided it best to speak to John Van den Kirkhoven, the Seigneur, himself. Not for nothing had O'Neil earned himself the soubriquet of

'Infallible Subtle.' That evening, O'Neil sat down to write to the King, to inform him of all that had transpired that day.

'Following what the servant told me, I visited my wife's kinsman, the Seigneur, and discussed the matter with him. He gave me a very sympathetic hearing and, in consideration of your Majesty, has given me his assurance that no action of his will result in the banishment of Mistress Barlow.

'It were well if Your Majesty commanded Mistress Barlow to deliver the child unto whoever you will appoint. I know from the Lord Taaf's letter that Your Majesty considers nothing but Mistress Barlow's sufferings and the next money you can get or borrow shall be sent to supply her.'

He lost no time in sending the letter to the King, who was more than grieved to receive it.

* * *

'I am tiring of Holland,' said Lucy one day to Ann.

'Since we have returned from England, I find the place does not hold the same appeal for me. I think I would like to live in Brussels for a while. It would be so good for Jamie and Mary to learn the language and mix with other people. Besides, Holland holds too many painful memories for me now.'

'Not enough Cavaliers for a start and too many people know too much about you here, my lady,' thought Ann, but she said nothing to betray her thoughts. Instead, she replied, 'I hear His Majesty is in Bruges.'

'How would you know that?' flashed Lucy.

'Just something I heard in the market,' said Ann.

Lucy's eyes narrowed. The servants could sniff out gossip quicker than the pigs could snuffle truffles from the ground.

Before the summer was over, Lucy, Ann and the children took up residence in a fine apartment in Brussels, looking down on a tree-lined street which led to an open square. The move was good for Lucy, bringing the roses back to her cheeks and the sparkle to her eyes. As she sat by the window one afternoon, watching the leaves on the trees shaking off the raindrops from the recent shower, women's voices and footsteps could be heard outside the door. There was a light tap on the door, then Ann's head appeared.

'May I show a lady into the day salon, Madam? Lady Bowles, Madam!'

Lucy knew the name and knew of the lady. To be more precise, Lucy knew Sir Charles Bowles very well, but his wife not at all. She had not had wives calling on her before. Gentlemen callers who visited her were usually discreet enough to conceal their liaisons from their wives.

'Show the lady in, Ann.'

There was nothing for it, but to go and face the woman, Lucy thought. She would tell her that she had not forced her husband to visit her, he had come of his own free will.

Lady Bowles was a lady of middling years, a little bit plump, a little bit plain, but possessed of a sweet nature. She chose to speak first. 'Mistress Barlow, forgive me for calling without prior notice today, but I was passing and, on an impulse, decided I must have a word with you.' Lucy's heart sank. She did not want trouble with this woman. If necessary, she would call Ann to show her the door. But what Lady Bowles had to say came as a surprise to Lucy.

'I have come to discuss a delicate matter. I do not quite know how to put this to you. Oh, dear, I am doing this very badly and dithering again.' She took a delicate lace handkerchief from her bag and patted her hot cheeks.

'You see, my dear, not to put too fine a point on things, I am getting older but my husband does not realise this. I have lost interest in that side of married life, but he has not. Do I make myself plain?' Lucy was beginning to understand what Lady Bowles was having so much difficulty in saying, but still the picture was not clear. Lady Bowles spoke again, 'What I have come to ask you is, might my husband call on you sometime? He does not know that I intended calling on you, and we have not discussed the matter, but it would be such a relief to me if he could call on you sometimes. I would feel free of some of my wifely duties then.'

When Ann had shown Lady Bowles out, Lucy sat down in the chair and laughed until the tears were steaming down her face. It was all she could do to keep a straight face while the woman was talking. Poor Lady Bowles, so innocent, trying desperately hard to be fair to her husband, understanding so little of the ways of the world. Lucy shook her head ruefully. Sir Charles Bowles had been one of her first callers when she had arrived in Brussels.

Very soon, news of Lucy's nightly visitors spread. Her name was on the lips of all Charles's Cavaliers and she was the toast of the town. Sir Edward Hyde, who was in Brussels, had received reports of Lucy's activities, which stirred a sense of outrage in him. He poured out his anger in a letter to the Marquis of Ormond, who was attending the King in Bruges.

'There is much talk here of a certain lady, very shrewd discourses, which will quickly get into England; I pray let her go to some other place.' But, for the moment, there was nothing the Marquis of Ormond, or anyone else for that matter, could do about Lucy, and if she had been asked to leave Brussels, she would have been very unwilling, for she was enjoying herself too much to contemplate leaving.

Of the Cavaliers who visited Lucy, the youngest was a mere Lieutenant, but she liked him much better than the others. He was blond and smooth skinned, with hardly a hair on his body and he reminded her of a boy she had known, once, long ago, in Dyfed. Lucy was careful to entertain only the men who appealed to her, so always the pleasure was mutual, but with Henry Grey, Lucy had a deeper satisfaction.

One night, when the young Cavalier had withdrawn from her body and fallen into a deep sleep by her side, on an impulse, Lucy wrapped him in Mary's old shawl and tied a diaper over his hips. Then she cradled him in her arms and sang a lullaby, until he opened puzzled eyes to look at her. She held his glance, until understanding dawned on him.

'Lucy, what in Heaven's name is this game we are playing?'

'Go back to sleep, Baby. Shush, shush,' she admonished.

So Henry Grey, all six feet of him, put his thumb in his mouth and pretended to fall asleep again. This was a special game that Lucy played only with her special Cavalier. Sometimes, Lucy was the good mother, but often she was the cross, bad mother who smacked her baby when he deserved it.

One evening, the game took a different turn.

'Mamma cross, cross tonight, Baby.'

Baby cried, then, through his tears, asked, 'Why is Mamma cross, cross?'

'Naughty Tom Howard in town. Naughty Tom Howard lock Mamma up in big, nasty Tower of London.'

Baby cried tears as big as October cabbages before asking, 'What Mamma want Baby to do to nasty Tom Howard?'

'Baby stab Tom Howard hard and kill him dead, dead.'

Then Mamma took a comforter and put it in Baby's mouth and wrapped her dear baby in the shawl and hummed him to sleep.

On 27th, August, 1657, Sir Edward Hyde, writing from Brussels, hastily despatched a letter to Sir Edward Nicholas, who was with the King at Bruges, to inform him of the latest scandal and outrage. The letter was short and pithy and came quickly to the point. It began, 'Tom Howard was stabbed on Friday last by a kinsman or servant of Mistress Barlow.'

Sir Edward's face was grave when he read the contents of the letter. He had no choice but to show it to the King. Charles read the letter, thanked Sir Edward, but made no comment. He would make up his own mind about the care and upbringing of Jamie, without pressure from his advisers.

When he was sure in his own mind that he had come to the right decision, then he would act.

Charles had been following the career of Arthur Slingsby, a Captain in the Guards, and was pleased with the way the man was making out. To show his appreciation, he created him a baronet. It was good to encourage young officers and rewards were a means of keeping morale high; a happy army ensured loyalty to the cause. So it was Sir Arthur Slingsby, whose stock was running high with the King, who was commissioned to snatch James, the future Duke of Monmouth, from the arms of his mother.

Vile nights are wont to be the father of vile deeds. Slingsby's orders were to remove the child from his mother with as little disturbance as possible. The King had not explained how best this might be done and if anyone had ever bothered to consider whether or not it was, indeed, possible to forcibly take a child, against the wishes of both mother and child and not cause a commotion, Slingsby had not been informed. Darkness was a necessary accessory to this bold deed and when night dropped a fog thick enough to shroud a man in, the baronet deemed nature could only assist his task. The chosen hour was early evening, for any later and he might discover a lover had arrived before him. A woman, her maidservant and two young children presented no serious impediment that might prevent him achieving his object and so it was with confidence that Arthur Slingsby climbed the stairs and rapped the door loudly. A man on the King's business had no need for polite taps. Ann Hill opened the door.

'Take me to your mistress,' he commanded, brushing the woman aside.

'One minute,' cried the maid in a vain attempt to stop him. 'Gentlemen enter here by invitation only,' but the soldier was not listening.

'Where is the boy?'

The boy did not appear, but his mother, in a state of undress, wearing only a peignoir of the sheerest material and a pair of satin slippers. She had caught sufficient of the conversation to alarm her.

Recognising the uniform of a Cavalier, she was in no doubt that this gentleman was not there to while away the hours of darkness in her arms.

'Who are you and what is your business?' she enquired with as much authority as her state of undress would allow her.

'I am here on His Majesty's business and I have been charged to remove the King's son to a place of safety.'

'On whose instructions?'

'The instructions of the King. Now stop wasting my time and lead me to the boy.'

Through clenched teeth, Lucy spat, 'Get out of here.'

'Mamma, Mamma,' wailed Jamie from an adjoining room.

In three strides, Slingsby covered the length of the room and pushed open the bedroom door, where the terrified child was huddled beneath the bedclothes.

'I'll get out when I have the child,' and the Captain leaned down and attempted to lift the boy, but Lucy was behind him and from the corner of his eye, he saw something bright and sharp gleaming in her hand. Grasping her wrist tightly, he forced the silver paper knife out of her hand.

'I'll thank you not to stab me in the way Tom Howard was stabbed.'

As the knife dropped from her hand, he kicked it under the bed. Too strong for her he might have been, but she was too resourceful for him. As he turned to lift the struggling Jamie again, Lucy picked up the brimming chamber pot and crashed it down on the soldier's head. The blow sent him reeling and he staggered against the wall, dripping wet. He still expected to win the contest. Defeat had not crossed his mind.

Neither of the adversaries in this duel were aware that a third person had joined them.

'Bravo, Mistress Barlow.'

Lucy's blond Cavalier lounged nonchalantly against the door, as beautiful and gilded a youth as ever decorated a Hilliard miniature. It was fortunate that he had come garbed in his stuffed and quilted pourpoint to witness the velitation and not in his soldier's uniform, for he and the Captain were unknown to each other and he was thus able to act with impunity towards his senior officer. Grabbing Sir Arthur by the shoulder, he addressed him in a most ungallant manner, 'Get the hell out of here, sirrah, before I run you out of town.'

'I'll have you know you are addressing His Majesty's representative.'

'I don't care who the hell you are; kidnapping is against the law. Get out or I'll have you in the Bastille,' and he forced him through the door and down the stairs, where a trail of drips recorded his passage. To the throng of gapers who had gathered from the other apartments to crane their necks, he said, with a shrug of his shoulders, an airy wave of his hands and the most charming smile, 'Il y a un accident, just a little accident.'

News of the brouhaha concerning the foreign lady, the Cavalier, the young gentleman and the chamber pot spread, fast as a crop of boils on a beggar's back, across Brussels. The story was on everyone's lips. Some thought it was the funniest story they had ever heard, others thought it was scandalous. Why was the lady only half-dressed at that time in the evening? Why had the young gentleman called on a woman without a husband? Why was an English baronet attempting to remove a young child from a poor, hapless woman. There were many versions of the story — it was Sir Arthur's child by the King's wife, it was the maid's child by Sir Arthur. There were as many different stories and twists and turns to the tale as there were tongues to wag it.

Lord Castlehaven and Monsieur Berkley set off to give the King their version of the story, in the manner of the chicken who went to tell the King the sky was falling down, in the nursery story. Sir Giles Mottet found that his duties in

Liége prevented him joining the procession to tell the King of the scandal, but he wasted no time in writing to inform the Marquis of Ormond that the two excellent gentlemen had departed that very day for the King's Court. So outraged was the good gentleman, so offended were his sensibilities by what he had heard, that he was loath to repeat the particulars of the shameful proceedings. The Ambassador, Don Alonzo de Cardenas, had written to the King to inform him that the ordinary people had found the action barbarous, abominable and most unnatural.

'The worst of it was, Sir Arthur doth say to all that the King hath given him order for it.'

Though a Cavalier Colonel had failed to get the better of Mistress Barlow, a Doctor of Divinity was inspired by the belief that Heaven would smile more favourably on his attempt to snatch the infant from his mother. Alas, he too came to learn that he was no better than other mortals and despite his most valiant efforts, he came to grief. Colonel Blank Marshall, a spy in the pay of Cromwell wrote, reporting the latest debacle, to the Lord Protector, 'There was another combat between Madam Barlow and Doctor Floid. He got the worse of it and is gone for Holland.'

* * *

Despite Lucy's fears over Jamie's safety, her appetite for pretty, costly, baubles did not diminish.

'Ann, I want you to go out and buy me perfume and some lace to tie in my hair,' she said one morning.

The servant took the money she was given and went off muttering to herself. They were already in debt to the butcher and she hoped she did not meet him when she was out, for she did not want to be told to remind her mistress of what she owed him again. It was she who got the abuse when Lucy kept tradesmen waiting weeks for their dues. Her mistress received as many visitors as ever and no doubt they paid her well, but, as always, she must have the luxuries before the necessities.

* * *

It was only a short while before Brussels was buzzing again with the latest gossip. Mistress Barlow's two children were with the King. There had been no kidnap attempt this time. Fate had played into the hands of His Majesty. Lucy Barlow had been imprisoned for debt. Everyone had seen it coming, of course. There were ever so many people who could talk of her extravagance, her love for the costliest perfumes, the best silks, the finest, tenderest cuts of meat. The tradesmen were the most indignant of all, yet they were the people who had allowed her to run up enormous bills, who had sought her patronage most assiduously of all. The King had taken pity on Mistress Barlow and paid her debts, on the condition that she would allow him the care of the children and this she had done. Respectable society had never known a lady like Mistress Barlow, around whom a new scandal blew as regularly as the tide came in and out. What they would have done to while away the idle hours if Mistress Barlow had not been in Flanders, they did not stop to consider.

Chapter 9

'Dansez-vous, Mademoiselle?'

Lucy looked up into the blackness of the eyes of a dark-skinned sailor whom she had noticed entering the dimly lit room earlier. He had been distinguishable by the white gash that ran from the outer corner of his eye down to his jaw-line. There was laughter in his eyes and they gleamed brightly as the golden loop in his ear lobe. He was not the sort of man she was used to, but the time for picking and choosing had gone.

'Merci,' she murmured, taking his outstretched hand. The rules had changed now, and no one meant what they said anymore. Many of the men who used this bar in the artists quarter of Montmartre, did not even bother with the nicety of dancing first. In the corner of the room, a trio of gypsies from Budapest was playing a haunting tune, a melody that Lucy did not know, but she recognised it as a song about lost love. A gypsy woman began to sing, her high pitched voice bringing an air of sadness to the refrain. Out of the corner of her eyes, Lucy watched her twisting her body in a lithe and sensuous way, her hair a dark, gleaming sheet down her back. She knew that there were men in that room who would kill for her, but she would have none of them, for she was the sister of the three fiddlers and she was the lover and mistress of each one of them. It was a blood relationship and they had killed men who tried to break into their ring of incestuousness. When their father had been alive, she had been his mistress, too. It was the gypsy way, the way they preferred.

Lucy was aware of the hairy, tattooed arms of the sailor holding her tightly and she found them comforting, in an odd way. She smelt the ship's oil on him, the tang of sea salt, the sharpness of peppers and sun-ripened tomatoes.

'Where do you come from?' She half expected him not to answer, for many of his type could not be bothered with talking, but he answered readily.

'I come from Santiago de Compostella.' Seeing a blankness in her expression, he smiled again. 'Ah, but you do not know Spain, non?' Lucy shook her head.

'Santiago is in the north west corner of Spain. We have a very important cathedral there, where all the Catholic Kings of Spain are crowned.'

Seeing the surprised expression in her eyes, he explained, 'My brother is a priest. I am the bad boy of the family. I ran away to sea and broke my mother's heart.'

'Have you been to Paris before?' enquired Lucy.

'Many times, but why haven't I met you before?'

They both laughed, but the gaiety had gone from Lucy's face, dark circles ringed her eyes and her prettiness was giving way to a haunted look.

The sailor had noticed Lucy on his arrival, then looked round for younger, prettier girls, but his eyes had gone back to Lucy, for there was something in the steadiness of the glance, the stillness of her manner, that fascinated him.

'Who are you? No, do not tell me, let me guess. A French princess who has forgotten her way to the Palais Cardinale? Or are you Cinderella, waiting for the clock to strike midnight?'

Lucy acknowledged he was amusing, but her heart was not in it. Since her release from prison, she had found herself penniless, with nowhere to go to rest at night but a doorway in a dark alleyway or the meannest of rooms.

'Come Querida!' he whispered, and she followed him through a side door and then up some stairs, till they found themselves on a landing. A bedroom door was open a crack and a thin shaft of light made out the figures of two men. Both had their backs to the door; the one nearest the door was twisting the arm of the other and pushing him onto the bed.

'In here,' and the Spaniard indicated a back bedroom, sparsely furnished, but not unpleasant.

Later, he smoked a clay pipe and they lay watching the smoke swirl up to the ceiling.

'Do you always stay here when you are in Paris?' Lucy wanted to know.

'Usually, if there is room. I have not seen you here before, though.'

'I have not been here before this evening.'

'A girl like you should be married, looking after your home and children. What are you doing in a place like this?'

'I-I was married. My husband was a French miner. He died in an accident.'

The sailor grunted. These girls were all the same, never telling the truth, looking for easy money. He didn't blame them, that was life, but this one was different, but how, he did not know.

'It's getting late. Where are you staying tonight.?'

She hesitated before answering, so he assumed she had nowhere to go.

'Do you want to stay here tonight? Si?'

Lucy had no idea where she might go after leaving the bar. If she stayed with the sailor, at least she would be safe for the night.

'Would you mind?'

'No me parece bien, it suits me.'

* * *

In England, people were wearying of Cromwell's Model Army of 'Saints', of disrupted Sundays when soldiers barged into their homes to check the Sabbath was being kept or

Parliamentary fasts observed. The Act of Parliament the populace hated the most was the one that punished adultery with death and even Puritan juries expressed their disgust by refusing to convict.

The Marquis of Ormond wondered if the time was ripe for a Royal invasion.

'Take Daniel O'Neil with you and go to London. Listen to the people talking in the taverns and on the streets. Do not tell the Lord Protector that I will marry his daughter, though. I did not like that idea of yours.' There was a twinkle in Charles's eye; even when men displeased him, he was never cross for long and usually saw the funny side of things.

'Poor Frances Cromwell. She must have shivered with fright when told of your idea of bringing peace to England. Here I am, known as the greatest philanderer on the Continent, and she a young virgin, for all I know, who says her prayers three times a day and again before going to bed,' and Charles laughed at his own wit.

Although Ormond and O'Neil's visit was meant to be secret, it soon reached the ears of the Protector that spies were in the city.

'An old friend of yours, the Marquis of Ormond, is in town, lodged at the Papist surgeon's, in Drury Lane,' remarked one of his major-generals. Cromwell was not entirely bereft of a sense of humour and allowed himself a wry smile, remembering Ormond's attempts at match-making.

'You had better tell him to be gone, I think. It is not fit that there should be a plot of this kind every winter.'

Charles took the return of the erstwhile spies philosophically. Besides, he had other things to occupy his mind, like the entertainments given by his aunt, Ann of Austria, who loved gaiety almost as much as Charles. At one of her balls, Charles fell hopelessly in love with Hortense Mancine, the beautiful niece of Cardinal Mazarin.

'I have only to look into the violet depths of your eyes and all other women cease to exist for me,' he whispered gallantly to her one night, as they stood on a balcony looking out over Paris.

'Mon Dieu!' the girl exclaimed. 'You say that tonight, but tomorrow, pouf, you have forgotten every word, even what I look like,' and she tapped his chest in mock reproval with her fan. To demonstrate the ardour of his passion, Charles swept her in his arms and kissed her lips fiercely, but she drew away and refused to take him seriously. She knew all about the loves of the English King, of the great love of his life, the Welsh woman, Lucy Barlow, of the years he had spent loving her and every other pretty woman who was in sight at the time. Charles could be pleasant company, but as a husband, King or not, she did not want him.

This was one occasion when Charles could not believe the lady meant what she said. He took his thwarted love to the Cardinal and explained he would love his niece until his dying day. Mazarin, wily old fox that he was, had prepared himself for this visit, for he had not failed to notice how the Dowager Queen's nephew followed every move his niece made and kept his eyes glued to her like limpet shells.

'Your Majesty, a King like you must not even think of marrying a niece of mine, for she is not royal and you must make a dynastic marriage. Your cousin, Henriette of Orange, would be privileged if the honour of being your wife fell to her.'

When Charles seemed to accept what he said, Mazarin folded his hands complacently over his stomach. His niece had told him she could do better for herself than marry a monarch without a throne.

But Hortense's attractions faded away quickly when Charles set his eyes on Beatrix de Cantecroix, the beautiful mistress of the Duke of Lorraine, which made her all the more desirable in his eyes. She was that most fascinating of creatures, the experienced woman, and he met her when his cousin, Philippe, invited him to a play at the Louvre.

Philippe, Louis's brother, had given his patronage to a

company of actors, known as Le Troupe de Monsieur, founded by Molière, the brilliant playwright who had formerly made Louis's bed, in his capacity as valet tapissier du roi. Molière had sold his hereditary privilege and used the money to finance his actors. 'Le Medecin Amoureux' was one of his best farces, though short. It was at the grand ball following this performance that Charles fell hopelessly in love with Beatrix.

As they danced, Charles thought he would lose himself in the deep beauty of Beatrix's eyes. What hidden delights she could initiate him into, what secret rituals she could teach him. He would forsake all others if the fascinating Beatrix could be his alone. As Charles led her into the Coranto, he felt her move with the grace and confidence of a pampered pet, for whom the costliest titbits were saved. Beatrix expected to be smoothed and petted, to have her maids brush her hair night and morning, her bath scented for her to slip into, her women holding a warm towel for her when she stepped out, her body rubbed with oils and costly spices.

When Beatrix laughed, she chuckled throatily and threw her head back, so that Charles admired her beautiful, creamy neck, smelt her scented breath and thought her parted lips were inviting him to kiss her, but she moved her head away from his and he saw the mockery in her eyes. It was only for the Duke of Lorraine that her eyes darkened with desire, only for him that her breath came faster, but still she found it fun to tease Charles mercilessly. Sometimes he thought she was on the verge of saying 'Yes', but then she turned her back and said he must go home. Beatrix enjoyed nothing so much as exercising her power over poor, besotted Charles. Eventually, he realised she had no intention of loving him, so Charles took himself off to Holland and began earnestly courting his cousin, Henriette.

Henriette of Orange was not displeasing to look at, but after the extravagantly beautiful Beatrix, she appeared very young, very innocent.

The Dowager Princess of Orange would not have

considered Charles a suitable match for her darling daughter, had not news come from England that Oliver Cromwell, thought by some to be immortal, had died.

In the Dutch Republic, people were overjoyed and danced in the streets to celebrate the death of 'the Devil'.

'It is a well known fact that the King has a Welsh mistress, the mother of his child. All men have their faults, but when Charles is married to my daughter, he will leave his behind,' the Dowager Princess remarked to her lady-in-waiting.

The thought of her daughter being the Queen of England was a most delightful prospect and already she was planning the wedding in her mind when information arrived that Richard Cromwell had climbed into the saddle vacated by his father and Parliament had no plans to recall Charles. This came as a shock for Henriette's mother, who immediately informed Charles the match could not go ahead. As for Henriette, she shed no tears, for she had not loved Charles and the overwhelming emotion she felt when he left Holland was one of relief.

* * *

When Lucy could find no customers in the city, she sometimes drifted down to the banks of the Seine, where trade of the roughest sort was to be had. Her Spanish sailor had left Paris, advising her to go back to wherever she came from, to leave the shameless city that was the fleshpot of the world. But there was no way out of the purgatory in which she found herself enmeshed, where truth was an outlaw, faith had perished and love was scorned. If she could have returned to the people who were her own sort, she would have, but there was nowhere to go where anyone cared for her anymore. Lucy was frail now and only her beautiful eyes and bones remained to remind the world of the lovely woman she once had been.

Caterine lived in one of the backstreet slums; she was only nineteen, but had been on the game since she was thirteen. One night, when the mists blowing over the embankments chilled the bones, Lucy was troubled by a hollow, barking cough. Though she had stood for a couple of hours, only one customer had stopped, paying her just what she asked, no more. No tips came her way now, though her fee was miserably low. Caterine could see how ill Lucy was this particular night.

'Come with me tonight and you can sleep on the kitchen settle. It is the best I have to offer, but at least it will be better than sleeping rough. We will go now, for I do not think either of us will have any more customers tonight.'

Lucy gratefully accepted her offer and accompanied her to a tenement block, grim and austere in the moonlight. Caterine went round to the back of the block and let them into a small kitchen, cold and squalid. Leading off from the kitchen was a tiny, box-like room, Caterine's bedroom.

Lucy had not been asleep more than half an hour, when she heared movement in the room. Sleepily, she sat up, remembering slowly that she was staying with Caterine.

'Caterine,' she called 'Caterine,' but there was no reply, for it was not her friend who disturbed her. Crouched by the door was the occupant of the room opposite Caterine's. Regarded by some as a simpleton, he possessed a low cunning; had he been a hunter, he would have marked out the weakest members of the herd immediately. He had seen Caterine enter the building with Lucy, then he had later seen Caterine slip out quietly to make more money before the night was over. Lucy was going to be easy meat for him. He would not have contemplated attacking Caterine, for her screams would have woken all the sleepers in the building. Sensing an intruder was in the room, Lucy sat upright, too terrified to scream or even to move.

Lucy was very light and frail and it was an easy matter to drag her onto the floor and take what he could. In a matter of minutes, it was all over and he had gone, taking what little pride she had left, together with her threadbare purse. In the darkness, Lucy cried softly, pulling the rags that served as blankets around her, but they gave no comfort. She could not bear to wait in the house any longer, and realising Caterine was not there, Lucy climbed out through a side window.

* * *

Charles was in that sanguine mood that often descends on people who have enjoyed a good meal and a bottle of claret to wash it down. First he chased the moths that circled the flames of the candles around the table, then he sat down on the floor and sang one of his favourite songs, 'I love my love with an 'A' because she is affable.' Edward Hyde rolled the Bordeaux round his mouth. That was the King's fault, too affable, too ready to oblige, too willing to forgive his enemies. He had pleaded with him many times not to be so kind, but His Majesty would not change his nature. If Hyde could be certain that Willis was a double agent, he would tell the King, who would probably take no notice of his warning anyway. When Charles had finished his song, Sir Richard Willis, one of his Majesty's favourite confidants, spoke, 'I hear Lucy Barlow has been seen on the streets of Paris, as part of the night life, if you understand my meaning.'

Willis watched Charles slyly, but if the King felt any pain, he showed no reaction, only turning his weary eyes to watch the flames flickering in the fire and if he thought of a love that had long ago consumed itself, only he knew.

* * *

King Louis XIV's passion for beautiful women was matched only by his love for ballet. Several times a week the French Court enjoyed an extravagant spectacle and if Louis took part, everyone enjoyed it even more. Louis excelled in his part as the 'Man of Ice' in his favourite ballet, 'The Festivals of Bacchus'. In the final scene, Apollo appeared, flattering Louis with his poetry and music.

Henrietta Maria sat with Minette, a smile on her face. Her nature was generous enough for her to be happy for her nephew and to acknowledge his success as a man and a King. She whispered to her daughter, 'Your cousin Louis is a great King. Already, his reign is exceedingly brilliant and he will go on to even greater splendour. My father was a great King; men have not forgotten Henri le Grand, but it is Louis's name that will be remembered. When men speak of France, they will speak of the Sun King, Le Roi Soleil.'

Minette smiled fondly at her mother and kissed her cheek and patted her hand. The queen could afford to be magnanimous tonight, for her son, who had stood in the wings, waiting for years to be called centre stage, had heard that Richard Cromwell was ill at ease in the crown of Lord Protector and was ready to abdicate. After many years of wandering, it seemd the finger of destiny was beckoning the King.

'Charles is already on his way to Boulogne, ready to cross the Channel,' whispered Henrietta Maria to her daughter. 'He will enter England through Cornwall or Wales, followed by his army. At last, my son will have his rightful dues.'

Minette could see a tear glistening in the corner of her mother's eye. They had all suffered, but when Charles's moment came, they would forget their exile and be happy again.

'When I came to England to be your father's bride, the church bells rang, trumpets sounded and there was a glorious splash of pageantry all across London. That is how it will be when Charles rides triumphantly into England.'

Henrietta Maria spoke with the certainty of a prophetess. Minette hoped she was not mistaken in her visions.

Lucy had heard Cromwell was dead. With all her heart, she hoped Charles would be recalled by the English Parliament, to sit upon his throne. Each day saw Lucy a little weaker and she did not expect to be alive when Charles was crowned King of England. The disease that afflicted so many of those who lived in the night's shadows was well advanced with her. Some nights she had to will herself to find the strength to walk the streets.

The Spanish sailor was the kindest man she had met in her new life. Perhaps if she returned to the bar in Montmartre, she might see him again. Even if he spurned her, she wanted to look once more at the face of the man who had been so kind to her.

The lights of the bistro shone through the steamy windows and though she peered hard, she failed to see him. Pushing open the salon door, she heard a shout, 'S'en aller, go away,' and realised the barman was speaking to her. As she walked out, she heard the man say to the maid, 'She's dying on her feet. I don't want her in here, she'll do nothing for trade.'

Ruefully, Lucy shook her head. How could she blame him? What he said was true. It was beginning to rain, and she put her head down, not knowing where to go. Suddenly, a figure stepped out of a doorway, blocking her path; from his paint spattered clothes, she guessed he was an artist. Indicating to her to follow him, he led her through a door in an alleyway and up a flight of musty steps. He took his time on the steps, but when they reached the top, she was breathless. Pushing open a door he led Lucy into an attic studio. The first sensation she was aware of was the brilliant heat from the fire and she paused, allowing it to flood over her like a blessing. The man lit an oil lamp and some candles and the light threw into relief the tall, sculptural shapes of the potted plants that he had on every spare surface. Against the wall stacks of canvasses rested and a rag rug warmed the bare boards on the floor. On the hob, a pan of something savoury bubbled and a cat slept on a cushion in front of the fire.

'I do not charge very much,' said Lucy, breaking the silence.

The man turned to look at her then, and in the dimly lit room she could just make out his eyes, dark as chips of coal.

He must have been of middling years, but there was vigour and purpose in the movements, making him appear younger. His smile was slow. He had seen what had happened between Lucy and the barman in the bistro. He was a painter, not well off, but making enough. There had been the years when he had slept rough, scraping the rabbits and hedgehogs off the roads to stew when the wheels of carts had gone over them, stealing the odd chicken, living with indifferent health. Pulling the settle closer to the fire, he undid her threadbare cloak and hung it from a hook behind the door.

'Make yourself comfortable,' and he indicated the seating arrangement. Filling two bowls with stew, he sat at the table to eat his. Watching Lucy from the corner of his eye, it was clear she was very weak, putting the spoon to her mouth slowly, supping just a little at a time. When she had put some flesh on, he would paint her.

He wondered what nationality she was. Her French was spoken with only the slightest trace of a foreign accent, but she was not Continental; her skin was too light and her bones too small. A few weeks rest and he could be looking at a different woman. There were different forms of the disease and while her health might never recover fully, she could live for years. A portrait of this woman could make his name and make her the belle of Paris. He shrugged his shoulders. Always the dreamer.

'You French?' His question broke the silence.

She shook her head. 'Welsh'.

He would not bother her with any more conversation, for she was very tired.

'I have promised to meet a friend in a bar. I'll be back in an hour. You'll be safe here and you are not leaving until you are better.'

Lucy settled back on the cushions. For the first time in months, she felt secure. Time passed, she did not know how long, but she had been dozing. Her head throbbed and her cheeks were burning. A breeze might cool her. With what strength she had left, she opened a window.

Her eyes searched the heavens, seeking the Pole Star, wondering if her sailor was looking to the skies for his navigation. But there were no stars in the dark night, only the vast emptiness of space.

Her head was throbbing again, but when she closed her eyes, she saw her mother holding a bunch of wild flowers, plucking one and giving it to her.

When she opened her eyes, there was only the darkness of the night and the wind moaning. If she listened, she could hear Marie calling her, 'Liwsi fach, dewch 'ma, dewch 'ma, come here. Good girl fach, Liwsi, good girl fach,' just as she had when Lucy was young and had knelt on the floor with her head in her old nurse's lap and Marie had smoothed her cheeks and twisted her ringlets round her fingers.

'I tried to be good, Marie, but I wasn't good enough.'

A shiver wracked her body and then she flushed hotly again.

Soon Charles would be the king of a Protestant country, but in his heart, she believed he was like his Huguenot grandfather, Henri Quatre, with a soul large enough to embrace the Protestant and Catholic faiths. Her head sank into her hands, she was past thinking of Charles now, or anyone else, for she was too weary.

'Stella Maris, Star of the Sea, lead me home,' she whispered. 'Je suis fatigué, so tired,' and the wind rose and carried her prayer over the rooftops of Paris until it floated down to the Seine and out to sea.

* * *

'Elle n'est plus, she's gone,' repeated Charles incredulously.

'For some strange reason, I always believed I would die before Lucy, but now she is dead.'

Hyde's lips set tightly. He could see the King had never

completely stopped loving her. Lucy Walter had been his first great love and first love had a habit of lingering in the mind long after it had ceased to be vital to either of the lovers. It became sacrosanct in the memory, a matter of sentimentality which often stood in the way of practical affairs.

Hyde's expression hardened. No longer would the King be hounded by the scandalous doings of the woman whose life had become interwoven with his.

Glancing at Charles again, he saw a man, not yet thirty, whose face showed signs of strain, the hair under the periwig already greying. Hyde's thoughts went back to the Welsh woman. Perhaps if the King had not left her to go to Scotland, perhaps if their natures had been less passionate . . .

He could go on forever. All he knew was that for a brief moment in time, two brilliant meteorites met on a collision course, leaving a sparkling trail of efflorescence in their wake. When history was written, men would tell the story of Charles II and Lucy Walter, so that each succeeding generation learnt that once, long ago, these two met and loved.

completely stopped loving her. Lucy Walter had been his first great love and first love had a habit of lingering in the mind long after it had ceased to be vital to either of the lovers. It became sacrosanct in the memory, a matter of sentimentality which often stood in the way of practical affairs.

Hyde's expression hardened. No longer would the King be hounded by the scandalous doings of the woman whose life had become interwoven with his.

Glancing at Charles again, he saw a man, not yet thirty, whose face showed signs of strain, the hair under the periwig already greying. Hyde's thoughts went back to the Welsh woman. Perhaps if the King had not left her to go to Scotland, perhaps if their natures had been less passionate . . .

He could go on forever. All he knew was that for a brief moment in time, two brilliant meteorites met on a collision course, leaving a sparkling trail of efflorescence in their wake. When history was written, men would tell the story of Charles II and Lucy Walter, so that each succeeding generation learnt that once, long ago, these two met and loved.